Dynamic Women Dancers

The Women's Hall of Fame Series

Dynamic Women Dancers

Anne Dublin

Second Story Press

Library and Archives Canada Cataloguing in Publication

Dublin, Anne
Dynamic women dancers / by Anne Dublin.

(The women's hall of fame series)
Includes bibliographical references.
ISBN 978-1-897187-56-2

1. Women dancers—Biography—Juvenile literature. I. Title.
II. Series: Women's hall of fame series

GV1785.A1 D82 2009   j792.802'80922   C2009-900731-2

Edited by Alison Kooistra
Designed by Melissa Kaita
Cover photo and icons © istockphoto.com

Printed and bound in Canada

Second Story Press gratefully acknowledges the support of the Ontario Arts Council and the Canada Council for the Arts for our publishing program. We acknowledge the financial support of the Government of Canada through the Book Publishing Industry Development Program.

The author gratefully acknowledges the support of the Ontario Arts Council.

ONTARIO ARTS COUNCIL
CONSEIL DES ARTS DE L'ONTARIO

Canada Council   Conseil des Arts
for the Arts   du Canada

Published by
Second Story Press
20 Maud Street, Suite 401
Toronto, ON
M5V 2M5
www.secondstorypress.ca

The author may be reached at: adublin@sympatico.ca

Contents

To my dance teachers, and to Bronwyn Precious.

Introduction

When I was twelve years old, I saw my first ballet at the old Royal Alexandra Theatre in Toronto. When the curtain rose, I felt transported to another world, a fairy-tale land filled with magic and wonder. I was hooked on dance. I came to love the dances that told stories and the dances that didn't, the gorgeous costumes and scenery, the music played by a full orchestra. Most of all, I loved the strength and grace of the dancers.

But what I didn't realize then was that behind the seemingly effortless façade is an art that takes years of hard work and unstinting dedication to perfect.

The dancers in this book are all famous for their talent, but the obstacles they had to overcome in order to dance are not so well known: Alicia Alonso was almost completely blind; Anna Sokolow overcame her mother's fierce opposition; Pearl Primus fought against racism in the United States. These women all faced enormous challenges in order to dance.

You will read here about women involved in different forms of dance—ballet, modern, flamenco, and Bharatanatyam. These women come from all over the world—Canada, the United States, Cuba, Spain, Russia, and India. For the most part, they developed their art in the twentieth century, but their dance forms often originated hundreds or even thousands of years earlier.

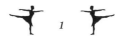

Today a lot of crossovers occur between dance types. Ballet dancers learn from modern dancers and vice versa. Even within one type of dance, there are different techniques and philosophies—but all dancers share the passion to communicate ideas and emotions through movement.

The dancers I've chosen to highlight in this book all had superb technique, but each developed her art in a different direction—from performance to teaching to choreography and even to social activism. Through their work, they inspired people to feel more deeply and to think more fully about what it means to be human. Through their honesty and courage, they showed that they could make a difference to the society in which they lived. Ruth St. Denis, a famous modern dancer, once said, "The great mission of the dancer is to contribute to the betterment of mankind." Each woman in this book accomplished this goal.

Dance is a living, breathing art. Just as you can't understand a piece of music or a painting solely through words, it's impossible to understand dance without seeing it. Watch a dance that was created or performed by one of the women in this book. It can be at a live performance, on DVD, or on the Internet. Only then will you get a real sense of the remarkable achievements of these dynamic women dancers. Maybe then you'll fall in love with dance, just as I did.

—Anne Dublin

Anna Pavlova

1881 - 1931

Bringing Ballet to the World

*M*argot Fonteyn, the great twentieth-century British ballerina, once wrote, "You can be sure that few mortals have, or ever have had, the mysterious, magical power of Pavlova, the 'Incomparable'—as she was justifiably called." Anna Pavlova had a special quality that made people all over the world idolize her. She transformed their lives.

Anna Pavlova was born in the city of Saint Petersburg, Russia, on January 31, 1881. She was born two months premature, a frail baby some people thought would not survive. Her mother, Liubov, worked as a laundry woman at the Maryinsky, the imperial theater in Saint Petersburg. Her legal father, Matvey, was a soldier in the army. He died when Anna was two years old.

Anna's real father was a wealthy Jewish businessman. Anna later confided to a friend that she didn't want people to learn about her Jewish father. She knew that being half-Jewish would have prevented her from following her dream to become a dancer, because there was a lot of anti-Semitism in Russia at the time.

Anna and her widowed mother were very poor. They lived in a tiny apartment and often had only rye bread and cabbage soup to eat. No matter where Anna's travels later took her, or how famous she became, she always loved plain Russian cooking: herring, *kasha* (porridge), black bread and butter, and pressed gingerbread.

Although she struggled to make ends meet, Liubov still tried to give her little girl an occasional treat. When Anna was eight years old, her mother took her to the Maryinsky Theatre (now the Kirov) for the first time. Anna saw the very first production of *The Sleeping Beauty*. She was captivated by Tchaikovsky's music, by the scenery, and by the costumes—but most of all by the dancing. She decided then and there to become a dancer. "It never entered my mind," she later said, "that there were easier goals to attain than that of principal dancer in the Imperial Ballet."

Anna had to wait two years, but when she was ten years old she tried out for one of the coveted places in the Imperial Ballet School. She knew that if she were accepted, her schooling would be paid for. Anna would learn to dance. That was all that mattered to her.

Anna wasn't typical of the other children who auditioned for the school. She was poor; they were rich. She was thin and delicate; they were stocky and strong. Nevertheless, something about Anna must have won over the examiners. She was accepted into the school.

Anna's body was different from the other girls' but it later became the ideal for ballet in the twentieth century. She had

a pale, oval face framed by smooth, black hair, dark, expressive eyes, and a long neck. Her legs were slender, without the slightest trace of bulging muscles (a common problem of bad training at that time), and her small feet were highly arched.

Although Anna had a good body for ballet, it wasn't perfect. For example, her big toe was longer than the others. When she went *en pointe*, it had to take the weight of her entire body. She sewed extra leather and thread onto the ends of her shoes in order to give her more support. (Today's pointe shoes are similar to Anna's, although they are twice as heavy.)

Being accepted into the school was only the first step in a long, arduous journey. The students wore uniforms, slept in dormitories, and led strict, regimented lives. They had one warm bath per week and otherwise washed in cold water. They had dance classes in the morning and academic classes—reading, arithmetic, history, and French—in the afternoon. The training was rigorous, but it produced dancers with superb technique. During her eight years at the Imperial Ballet School, Anna worked as if there were nothing else in the world that mattered.

When a young woman graduates from ballet school and is accepted into a ballet company, she usually begins on the lowest rung of the ladder, as a member of the *corps de ballet*. However, after Anna's stunning graduation performance in 1899, she was immediately promoted to the level of *coryphée*, a dancer who dances as part of a small ensemble with only two or three others. How happy Anna must have felt to be promoted so quickly!

It is a great compliment to a

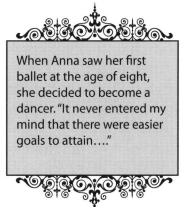

When Anna saw her first ballet at the age of eight, she decided to become a dancer. "It never entered my mind that there were easier goals to attain…."

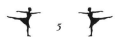

dancer when a choreographer creates a particular role for her. In 1900, Marius Petipa, the great Russian ballet master, teacher, and choreographer, created a special role for Anna: Frost in *The Seasons*. In 1902, when Anna danced the role of Nikiya in *La Bayadère*, one of Petipa's greatest ballets, her reputation became firmly established with critics and the public alike. This advancement was unprecedented in the super-competitive world of the Maryinsky Theatre.

That success was followed by another in 1903 when Anna danced the title role in *Giselle*. She became so popular that a group of fans called "Pavlovtzki" cheered her at every performance and crowded around the stage door to catch a glimpse of their idol.

Anna worked very hard to improve her technique and to strengthen her back and feet. In 1903, she went to Milan, Italy, to study with a retired ballerina, Caterina Beretta. After she returned to Saint Petersburg, she danced the ballerina roles in *Paquita* and *Le Corsaire*.

The dancers of the imperial theaters were generally insulated from the troubles in the world. They were treated like pampered pets. However, world events would soon have a profound effect on Anna's personal and professional life.

Various groups in Russia were coming into conflict at the turn of the century. Farmers, workers, and students demanded democratic reforms. They wanted freedom of speech and freedom of the press and were desperate to be liberated from the tyrannical rule of the tsar and his family. On a cold January morning in 1905, thousands of workers marched to the tsar's Winter Palace. The troops fired on the unarmed crowd. They killed more than one hundred people and wounded many more. This terrible massacre became known as "Bloody Sunday."

Strikes spread throughout Russia. Factories, schools, and hospitals closed. The country was in turmoil. Some of the members of the ballet company began to talk about the need for reforms in their own profession. For example, dancers often got choice roles not only because of their talent, but because of their connections with people in authority.

Anna and Michel Fokine, a rising young choreographer, became two of the leaders of this group. Many of the dancers went on strike. They demanded higher pay, a shorter work week, and the right to choose their company's manager.

The director refused to meet with them, but instead put pressure on the dancers to give up their demands. He hinted that they might lose their jobs if they didn't. Feeling great anguish, the dancers were forced to cave in. Although the protest fizzled out, Anna was convinced that they had fought for a just cause. She was labeled a "nonconformist" by the theater management. Nevertheless, soon after the strike ended, Anna was promoted to the rank of ballerina and was given the coveted role of Kitri in Aleksandr Gorsky's restaging of Petipa's *Don Quixote*.

Anna was rising rapidly in the company. In 1906, she was promoted again, this time to prima ballerina. In only six short years, she had gone from coryphée to ballerina. Not only was Anna making a good salary by then, but she was given a new pair of pointe shoes for each act of a ballet! Anna began to live well, even luxuriously. She rented an elegant apartment in a fashionable district of Saint Petersburg.

But Anna knew she still had more to learn. She hired Enrico Cecchetti, the great Italian ballet teacher, to give her private lessons. Cecchetti once said, "I can teach everything connected with dancing, but Pavlova has that which can be taught only by God."

Even though Anna was getting a ballerina's salary, she would not have been able to live in such comfort and pay for private lessons without extra support. Victor Dandré, a wealthy aristocrat, fell in love with Anna and became her patron. He worked on the city council and supported various charities, such as the Dance Committee of the Society for the Prevention of Cruelty to Children. This group raised funds by organizing and presenting ballet performances.

In 1907, Victor invited Michel Fokine to create two ballets for one of his charity events. Anna danced in both ballets. The year 1907 was important to Anna for another reason. In December, she danced a short piece called *The Swan*, choreographed by Michel to music by Camille Saint-Saëns. It soon became known as *The Dying Swan* and was Anna's most famous solo piece.

Anna was given permission to travel abroad, and in 1908 she began to perform in countries outside Russia. This was a privilege that very few Russian dancers received. Because they had been trained in the Imperial Ballet School, they were expected to perform at the Maryinsky Theatre for their entire careers.

Anna performed to great acclaim in several cities in northern Europe. In 1909, she repeated her success in other European cities. Later the same year she traveled to Paris, where she joined Sergei Diaghilev's new company of Russian dancers. She shone in two ballets choreographed by Michel Fokine: *Les Sylphides* and *Cléopatre*.

Anna next traveled to London where she danced before the king and queen of England. That was the first time she performed with Mikhail Mordkin, a dancer from Moscow. This handsome, talented man was a strong dancer, but he had a quick temper and was jealous of Anna's popularity.

Why did Anna want to travel so much? She admired the great nineteenth-century ballerina, Marie Taglioni, who had toured all over Europe and been adored by countless fans. But Anna was also passionate about bringing ballet to people who had never seen the art form. She once said, "I want to dance for everybody in the world."

In 1910, Anna danced in the United States for the first time at the Metropolitan Opera House in New York City. She captivated American audiences with her performance in *Coppélia* the first night, and *Bacchanale* and *Pas de Deux* the second night. Sol Hurok, an American impresario, said that Anna's first appearance in New York City was "the beginning of the ballet era in our country."

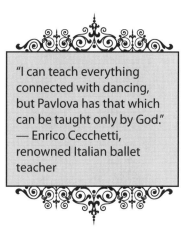

"I can teach everything connected with dancing, but Pavlova has that which can be taught only by God."
— Enrico Cecchetti, renowned Italian ballet teacher

Later that year, Anna danced for a three-month season in London at a music hall called the Palace Theatre. She became a favorite with audiences when she performed three *pas de deux*: *Valse Caprice*, *Bacchanale*, and the waltz from *Chopiniana*. Twelve other Russian dancers performed along with her, but Anna was the star. She also danced a number of solos including, of course, *The Swan*. Margot Fonteyn wrote that Anna could "transform herself into whatever she chose: a flower, a swan, a dragonfly …."

Anna loved touring, so in August 1910 she asked for permission to tour abroad for two more years. The director of the Maryinsky denied her request. Anna didn't accept that refusal. Instead, she paid a huge penalty to break her contract. In September of that year, she returned to the United States with Mikhail Mordkin and her own small company of twelve soloists.

In April 1911, they returned to London to begin another long engagement. But the jealous Mikhail wanted equal billing with Anna, and they had a serious argument about it. They made up, but Mikhail left the troupe before the end of the season. They never danced together again. (Mikhail eventually established a ballet school and company in the United States.

MEDINAH TEMPLE, CASS AND OHIO STREETS
MONDAY EVENING, FEBRUARY 28th, 8:15 o'clock

Fortune Gallo Presents

Mlle. Anna **PAVLOWA**

and BALLET RUSSE

A poster for Ballet Russes featuring Anna Pavlova

Alicia Alonso's husband, Fernando, danced in that company in the late 1930s.)

During the fall 1911 London season of Sergei Diaghilev's company, the Ballets Russes, Anna danced with Vaslav Nijinsky in *Giselle, Le Pavillon d'Armide, Cléopatre, Le Carnaval,* and the bluebird *pas de deux* from *The Sleeping Beauty.* It was magic to watch the most exciting ballet stars in the world dance together! However, after that short season, Anna never danced with Nijinsky again.

Anna didn't want to stay in Paris with Sergei Diaghilev's company. She wanted to travel all over the world with her own company. She wanted to choose the ballets, the costumes, and the music, rather than be under someone else's thumb—no matter how brilliant or popular that person was.

Anna and Victor, her wealthy patron, bought a house in London in 1912. Victor had become her constant companion and they eventually married. Ivy House was the one place in the world where Anna could retreat from her hectic life. She loved to plant flowers in the garden, watch the birds, and carve small sculptures. In her spacious studio, she taught ballet to English students. A few of these students eventually joined her company.

In 1913, Anna began to cut her ties with The Imperial Ballet. In 1914, she danced for the last time in her beloved Russia. She never returned to her country again. A bloody world war began in that year, and in 1917, a violent revolution tore her country apart. It would be years before Anna would see her mother again.

By the end of 1914, Anna had formed her own company—the Pavlova Ballet. Thirty-two dancers were usually in the company, as well as a ballet master, an orchestra conductor, musicians, wardrobe people, mechanics, stagehands, and electricians.

Victor acted as manager of the company. He made the

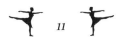

Anna Pavlova in *The Dragonfly*

bookings and all the travel arrangements. This was no mean feat. The company's dancers and baggage traveled in their own special train. The baggage was made up of about four hundred pieces of luggage, including forty heavy cases of scenery and more than one hundred costume hampers. There were more than two thousand costumes in all!

Throughout the 1920s, Anna and her company were constantly on tour. They took ballet to people who had never seen it before. They danced in opera houses, concert halls, meeting halls, and high school auditoriums. From North America to South America, from Europe to South Africa, from the Far East to Australia, Anna carried out her mission—to bring the joy and wonder of ballet to people all over the world. It is estimated that she journeyed three hundred and fifty thousand miles to four thousand cities during fifteen years of touring. And that was without the convenience of cars, buses, or airplanes!

Throughout her career, Anna never forgot what it felt like to be poor. She often gave special performances to aid various charities. Whether she was dancing in a concert for widows and orphans, for the wounded in World War I, or for the Red Cross, Anna was always concerned about people in need. Shortly after the war began in 1914, she said, "I can offer nothing but my art. It is a poor thing when such brave deeds are being done."

Anna was involved personally in a number of causes. For example, many people had been forced to run away from Russia after the 1917 Revolution. In 1921, Anna rented a house outside Paris, fixed it up, and furnished it as a home for exiled Russian refugee girls. She hired people to care for the girls. Although some people donated money to the home, Anna paid most of the expenses from her own pocket. By the time the home closed, some forty-five girls had found a refuge there.

In early 1931, when Anna was coming back from a short

holiday in France, she caught a chill. By the time she reached Holland, the starting point of her next tour, she had developed pneumonia. She died in the early hours of January 23, 1931. All over the world, people mourned her death.

Why was Anna Pavlova so important in the history of dance? It wasn't only because of her technique or because she had a gift for drama. Anna's power came from her incomparable stage presence, which moved and captivated audiences everywhere. She could make people smile or cry; she could make them forget about their troubles; she could give them hope.

Anna inspired many people to become dancers, teachers, or choreographers. People such as Agnes de Mille (United States), Alicia Markova (England), and Robert Helpmann (Australia) never forgot the times they saw Pavlova dance. Marie Rambert, founder of the Ballet Rambert in England, once said: "Her spirit came straight across the footlights and lit the world for us. We were not lookers-on—our souls were dancing with her."

On the night that Anna was supposed to have given her next performance, the audience sat quietly in the theater. The curtain opened onto an empty stage, lit by a solitary spotlight. As the music of *The Dying Swan* played, many people wept openly. The curtain closed. Anna Pavlova would never dance again.

Anna once wrote: "I desire that my message of beauty and joy and life shall be taken up and carried on after me.... If I have achieved even that little for my art, I am content."

Anna Sokolow

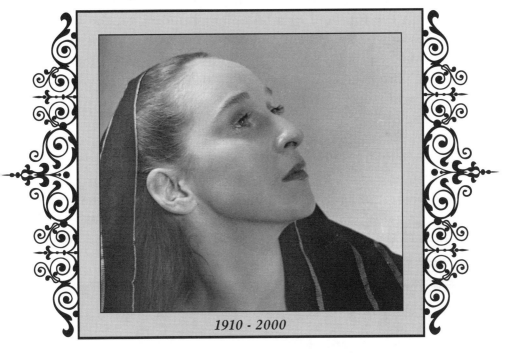

1910 - 2000

Immigrant to Innovator

People used all kinds of words to describe Anna Sokolow: tough, uncompromising, honest, risk-taking, intense, committed, and generous. Anna had to be tough, for her beginnings were far from easy. She was the child of poor immigrants, but she became one of the pioneers of modern dance in the United States, Mexico, and Israel.

Anna was born on February 9, 1910, in Hartford, Connecticut, to Sarah and Samuel Sokolow, who had emigrated a few years earlier from Pinsk, a city in Byelorussia in Eastern Europe. Anna had an older brother, Isadore (Izzy), an older sister, Rose, and a younger sister, Gertie.

The Sokolows were desperately poor. In 1912, they moved

to New York City, where Samuel hoped to find work. They lived on the top floor of a tenement building on the Lower East Side. The apartment had one large, narrow room, a tiny bedroom, and a bathroom they had to share with the other people who lived on the same floor. Because Samuel was ill with Parkinson's disease, he was eventually placed in a charity hospital.

Sarah was forced to earn a living as well as take care of her four children. She worked as a sewing machine operator in a garment factory. In addition, she got involved (as many East European immigrants did) in socialist, left-wing movements, such as her union, the International Ladies' Garment Workers' Union (ILGWU). She was determined to fight for better conditions for workers who slaved away in sweatshops.

Anna Sokolow in 1922

When Anna was about ten years old, the family moved again—this time to the Upper East Side. Because Sarah was so busy, she sometimes had to leave her children alone after school. She refused to let them play in the streets with other neighborhood kids. She wasn't always able to keep an eye on her children, but she wouldn't let them grow up wild.

Sarah sent Anna and Rose to a free cultural program run by the Emanuel Sisterhood. Anna took dance classes there in the style of Isadora Duncan, one of the pioneers of modern dance. The students wore flowing, Grecian-style dresses, waved filmy scarves around, danced barefoot, and expressed their emotions by moving to classical music. It was in these classes that Anna "fell madly in love with dancing."

Over the next few years, Anna learned everything she could about dance. At the age of fifteen, she went back to the Lower East Side to continue her training at the Henry Street Settlement House. She took classes in dance, mime, diction, and voice—one hour of each weekly—but that wasn't enough for Anna. She was determined to become a professional dancer and knew she would have to take more classes.

Her mother was horrified. She believed that it was proper for a "good Jewish girl" to become a teacher or a secretary, not a dancer. Anna remembered Sarah saying, "You mean, you are going to be a *kurvah* (prostitute)?" Anna replied, "No, Mama, I mean, I am going to be a dancer." Sarah told Anna to get out.

Anna dropped out of school and left home. Desperately poor, she supported herself by taking odd jobs, like working in a teabag

When Anna told her mother she was going to become a dancer, her mother threw the fifteen-year-old out of the house. Anna worked in a teabag factory and shared a loft with six others. They didn't have enough blankets to go around, so Anna slept in a laundry bag.

factory or as a model for the Art Students' League. She shared a loft apartment with six other young artists. There weren't enough blankets to go around, so Anna, who was the smallest person in the group, had to sleep in a laundry bag!

In 1928, when Anna was eighteen, she joined the Neighborhood Playhouse's new group, the Junior Festival Players, on a full scholarship. There she learned movement, singing, diction, and theater craft. Martha Graham, an important innovator of twentieth-century modern dance, was one of her teachers. In her early twenties, Anna also started taking ballet classes. The fact that Anna was getting such comprehensive training in dance techniques along with other theater-art forms would serve her well throughout her entire career.

In late 1929, Anna joined Martha Graham's new professional company. For most of the 1930s, she studied and danced with Martha. Anna was a slim, petite young woman with a strong body, blue-gray eyes, high forehead, and light brown hair. She was a powerhouse on stage. She could jump and turn like a dynamo, and she had a stage presence that people noticed.

Louis Horst, an accompanist and composer for Martha Graham's company, had a great influence on Anna's development as a choreographer. Anna eventually became his assistant, and worked with him until 1938. Louis taught Anna about music and dance forms, and encouraged her to explore her own ideas.

Anna's working-class upbringing and her mother's left-wing activities strongly influenced her dance creations. Instead of finding her inspiration in ancient myths and legends, Anna and others like her—in what was called the "radical dance" movement—looked to current world events for their ideas. Themes weren't hard to find.

The hard economic times of the Depression and the rising threat of fascism in Spain, Germany, and Italy were rich nuggets to mine. These young, idealistic choreographers, mostly from working-class backgrounds, insisted that dance was more than entertainment. They wanted to galvanize people to make changes in all spheres of life—social, economic, and political. Anna believed that "art should be a reflection and a comment on contemporary life," and that people need to be involved with the world around them to change society for the better. She said, "I felt a deep social sense about what I wanted to express, and ... the things that affected me deeply personally [are] what I did, and commented on."

Anna brought her dances to eager audiences at union meeting halls and at the settlement houses where new immigrants learned the language and culture of the United States. In 1933, Anna choreographed *Anti-War Trilogy*. During the 1930s, she explored similar themes in *Inquisition '36, Excerpts from a War Poem*, and *Slaughter of the Innocents*. However, even

The Dance Unit in *Anti-War Trilogy* (1934)

in her most heartrending works, Anna reminded her audience that the human spirit was strong and noble.

By 1933, Anna was the youngest American choreographer with her own professional dance company, which she called the Dance Unit. In 1936, she gave her first full evening concert at the 92nd Street YMHA in New York City. Anna's sister, Rose, designed and sewed the costumes. They worked together closely for years.

Even Anna's mother eventually came around. The story goes that when Sarah attended one of Anna's concerts, someone asked her to remove her hat. Sarah refused to do so because she said it was her daughter who was the star of the show.

Anna was true to her convictions even when it cost her chances to advance her career. She was against fascism and anti-Semitism, so in 1936 she refused to take her company to the International Dance Festival organized by the German Nazi government for the Olympics in Berlin. It would have been a chance to participate in a world-famous event, but Anna had no doubt about what she should do.

In 1939, Anna and her company were invited to Mexico with the aim of bringing modern dance to that country. They were an instant success. People clamored for tickets; performances increased from six to twenty-three. The run was wildly popular but, because of various problems, the members of the company earned almost no money. The exhausted dancers returned to New York while Anna stayed on for another eight months.

Anna had a new project—to create a Mexican modern dance company. This had developed by 1940 into "La Paloma Azul" (The Blue Dove)—a collaborative group of dancers, artists, and musicians. As a term of respect and affection, the fifteen women in the original dance group were nicknamed "Las Sokolovas" by a local newspaper. The name stuck.

Even though La Paloma Azul survived only one season, Anna's impact on the dance scene in Mexico was significant. Until well into the 1970s, she traveled between New York and Mexico City—sometimes every year, sometimes less often. She became known as "the founder of Mexican modern dance." Anna loved her time in Mexico. She commented that Mexican people "have a tradition of respecting art and whoever is involved in art is respected there. For the first time in my life, I knew what it felt like to be an artist."

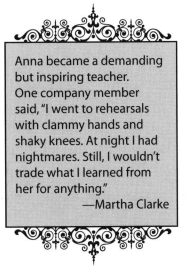

Anna became a demanding but inspiring teacher. One company member said, "I went to rehearsals with clammy hands and shaky knees. At night I had nightmares. Still, I wouldn't trade what I learned from her for anything."
—Martha Clarke

In Mexico, Anna met and fell in love with the artist Ignacio (Nacho) Aguirre. He made her feel accepted, beautiful, and desirable. They never managed to reconcile where they would live, for Anna needed New York to be her home base; Nacho, Mexico City. Fifty years later, long after they were no longer together, Nacho still had a photo of Anna in his living room.

Anna choreographed works based on Mexican and Spanish themes, for she had great respect for the rich culture and heritage of the Mexican people. Among these were: *Homage to García Lorca, Carmen*, and *Spanish Balcony*. By exploring themes important to Mexican people, Anna found the courage to explore her own Jewish history, religion, and culture.

Before Anna had gone to Mexico, she had choreographed only one work with clear Jewish content—*The Exile* (1939). The piece was divided into two parts: "I had a garden," describing the sweetness of Jewish life in pre-Nazi Europe, and "The beast is in the garden," describing the arrival of Nazism. In 1945, she created *Kaddish*, named after the mourning prayer recited when a person has died and on the anniversary of his or her death.

Years later, in 1961, Anna created *Dreams*, a masterwork that portrayed the desperation, helplessness, and anguish of the six million Jews who died during the Holocaust.

Anna explored other Jewish themes in her dances. She expressed her admiration for biblical women like Ruth, Miriam, and Deborah, and for historical figures like Hannah Senesh and Theodor Herzl. She helped stage huge extravaganzas in

Anna Sokolow in *Kaddish* (1945)

New York—a Purim Festival and Pageant at Madison Square Garden in 1952, and a Chanukah Festival in 1954 to raise money for the new country of Israel. Anna had rebelled against her Jewish upbringing when she left home at the age of fi.̃ ˜en; now she was finding the world of her childhood again, but ̃is time through her art.

In 1953, Jerome Robbins, one of America's leading choreographers, invited Anna to Israel. He had selected the Inbal Dance Theatre to represent Israeli dance abroad and he wanted Anna to work with the company.

Anna felt an immediate connection to Israel. She said, "I certainly didn't expect to be affected so deeply, but the minute the plane landed I was overwhelmed with an indescribable feeling about being there." Although Inbal's dancers had a strong sense of movement and rhythm, they had a long way to go before they could be considered professional. They needed to study technique in a disciplined way, to attend rehearsals regularly, and to learn how to behave backstage. For example, the dancers used to bring their families backstage during per-formances for tea and refreshments!

With toughness and passion, Anna taught modern dance and ballet to the Inbal group; she instilled in them the disci-pline she had learned many years ago when she had danced with the Martha Graham Company. She said: "I felt the enor-mous responsibility on my part ... to give them a kind of strength and an understanding of what they were and to help them project this more effectively."

Anna was undaunted by the poor working conditions and makeshift stages these young dancers had to endure. After all, she had faced similar challenges when she had created her company in the 1930s.

After three years of hard work, Inbal was ready to make its debut. Sol Hurok, the dance and theater impresario, orga-nized the company's tours to England and the United States.

Sara Levi-Tanai, Inbal's artistic director, had created works based on biblical themes, the landscape of Israel, and Yemenite culture. Audiences and critics alike were enthusiastic about dances such as *Yemenite Wedding* and *Song of Deborah*.

In 1962 Anna founded a new company in Israel, the Lyric Theatre. She wanted to create a company where acting and dancing would complement each other. She insisted that the dancers get paid a salary of about two hundred dollars per month. That wasn't a lot, even by the standards of the day, but it was the first time that working dancers in Israel were paid. Before that, the dancers had to work at other jobs to make ends meet. For example, one of the men was a mechanic; another, an elephant keeper in the Tel Aviv Zoo.

Anna's dancers had only three months to rehearse before they went on tour in a series of forty concerts. They performed in Tel Aviv, Haifa, and Jerusalem; they danced in *kibbutzim* and other settlements throughout the country. It was a grueling schedule and the heat was sometimes unbearable.

After the tour, the members of the group pleaded with Anna to make Israel her home base. But New York City was pulling her back as it always did. The Lyric Theatre managed without Anna as well as it could, but the company lasted only until 1964—a total of three seasons.

Whenever her schedule permitted, Anna traveled back to Israel to teach and choreograph. She did this for more than thirty years. She rarely earned a fee for her work, for she believed that, by donating her time, she could help the country she had come to love.

Meanwhile, Anna was displaying her prodigious talents on other stages, in shows that ranged from ballet to opera to Broadway. Because of her early training at the Neighborhood Playhouse, Anna also felt comfortable in the theater. Starting in the 1940s, Anna staged dances for shows on and off Broadway, the center of theater in the United States. These included

Leonard Bernstein's *Candide*, Franz Kafka's *Metamorphosis*, and James Rado and Gerome Ragni's *Hair*. Anna's most famous work for a ballet company, *Opus '65*, became the prototype of the "rock ballet." It perfectly expressed the alienation of 1960s youth.

Anna was an artist who always pushed boundaries. She was intrigued by the possibilities of using different art forms in a single work. For example, in 1951 she combined dance, mime, and the spoken word in *The Dybbuk*. Based on a poem by S. Ansky, *The Dybbuk* tells the story of a bride whose body is possessed by the spirit of her dead suitor. Over the decades, Anna continued to experiment with combinations of music, dance, mime, and acting in such works as *Act Without Words* (1969), *Magritte, Magritte* (1970), and *From the Diaries of Franz Kafka* (1980).

But things were never easy for Anna. In the late 1960s, she was plagued by dark moods. She had broken up with a young man with whom she had had a relationship; her mother, Sarah, and her brother, Izzy, had died; and she was taking medication for back pain that acted as a depressant. In early 1970, Anna spent several months in and out of hospital, where she was treated for severe depression.

Anna gradually recovered and began to work again. By 1971, she had created an important new work: *Scenes from the Music of Charles Ives*. Anna continued to choreograph until she was eighty-seven years old.

Anna was an innovative choreographer, but she was also an inspiring teacher to students all over the world—from the United States to Mexico, from Israel to Japan, from Canada to England. She taught both actors and dancers at the Juilliard School in New York for many years. Anna always insisted that her students have the courage to express their feelings directly and honestly in front of an audience—a difficult task. She was a tough, demanding teacher, and, when her students' work didn't meet her standards, she didn't hold back her ferocious criticism and quick temper.

Martha Clarke, one of the members of Anna's company, once said: "Every day that I worked with Anna I went to rehearsals with clammy hands and shaky knees. At night I had nightmares. Still, I wouldn't trade what I learned from her for anything."

Anna's works are in the repertoires of dance companies all over the world. She received many honors and awards during her lifetime—honorary doctorates, a Fulbright Fellowship, and the Samuel H. Scripps Award, to name only a few.

On March 29, 2000, Anna died at the age of ninety. She had approached life and dance with integrity and courage. She never cared if her work appealed to popular tastes or if she had much material success. She made people confront the difficult issues of her time with strength, dignity, and hope.

Carmen Amaya

1913? - 1963

Capturing People's Hearts

*I*n 1917, Carmen Amaya was a skinny, dark-haired Gypsy girl singing and dancing in the waterfront taverns of Barcelona, Spain, for the coins that people threw onto the floor. She would go from rags to riches more than once in her life, but she always remembered the heritage of her people. Because of her, flamenco dance was never the same again.

Carmen was born on November 3, 1913 (probably), in Somorrostro, a Gypsy squatter settlement of shacks and tents on a beach near Barcelona. The family lived in a wagon covered by a canvas roof. Carmen was born on a blanket under the wagon during an early winter storm.

Carmen came from a long line of Gypsy flamenco

Carmen was a powerful dancer. Although she was tiny, on more than one occasion her furious footwork broke through the floor!

performers. Her mother, Micaela Amaya Moreno, was a strong, quiet person. Although she was an excellent dancer, she danced only at private gatherings. Micaela had married at the age of fourteen and had ten children. Carmen was the second of six surviving children— four girls and two boys. Her father, José Amaya, known as "El Chino," was a flamenco guitarist. Like most of the Gypsies of Spain, Carmen's family lived in desperate poverty. They scrabbled to make a living any way they could. Micaela sold linens; José bought and sold used clothing.

From the time she was little, Carmen loved to dance. When she was three years old, she would dance on the wagon while her mother brewed coffee and her father played his guitar.

People who know about flamenco say that the true female flamenco dancer, the *bailaora*, learns her art from early child-hood; that, although other people can learn to dance flamenco, only a person who is nurtured by flamenco from an early age can dance it in a pure and authentic way.

Carmen learned the art of flamenco from her mother and from her aunt, as well as from important dancers of the day, such as La Macarrona, La Malena, La Tanguera, and La Salud. What was unusual for the time was that she also learned the fast footwork of the male dancer from her father and a fam-ily friend, Raphael (also called "El Gato"). Although Carmen learned from other people, she developed her own style at an early age. Her sister said, "She danced as she felt and no one told her to do it any other way."

Carmen began dancing professionally at the age of four. Around midnight, she and her father would venture out of their camp into the rough nightlife districts of the town.

Carmen would dance in a *tablao* (tavern or bar) while El Chino played the guitar. The customers were mostly local people and dockworkers.

They would come back to their camp around dawn. El Chino demanded nothing but the highest standards from his talented daughter, pushing her to practice up to six hours a day. El Chino was an energetic, intelligent man who would direct Carmen's career for much of her life. He arranged Carmen's bookings and later used her earnings to help support the family.

Although it was against the law for such a young child to work, Carmen continued to dance because the family was destitute; she said later that she was "spurred on by gnawing hunger." When she was four years old, the police raided one tablao where she was performing. She later recalled: "My father ran for a taxi to have waiting at the stage door, and I ran backstage looking for a hiding place. You'll never guess where I hid—under the overcoat of the *cantaor* [singer] José Cepero! He was a big man and I a tiny tot, and he held me inside his coat with one hand while the police searched in vain."

By the time she was seven years old, Carmen's fans were calling her "La Capitana" (The Captain, or Leader). People soon recognized Carmen's genius for flamenco dance. Agustín Castellón, "Sabicas," a famous guitarist, described the first time he saw Carmen dance: "It seemed like something supernatural to me.... I never saw anyone dance like her. I don't know how she did it, I just don't know!" Carmen was about ten years old.

Carmen was now earning enough money to help support the family, and soon they settled in their first house. Carmen's father built it out of adobe (mud bricks). There was only one big room, divided into a kitchen and a bedroom.

When Carmen was about eight years old, she went with her aunt, an acclaimed flamenco dancer known as "La Faraona,"

and her mother's cousin, Maria, known as "La Pescatera," to Paris to perform in a show led by a popular singer called Raquel Meller. Carmen completely stole the show. Meller was so jealous of Carmen's popularity that she fired her.

Sometime around 1928, when Carmen was a teenager, the family left Somorrostro and moved into a better house in Barcelona. In 1935, they would move again, this time to Madrid.

Carmen has been called a genius because she revolutionized the style of women's flamenco dance. Before Carmen's time, the female dancer stressed movements from the waist up, movements of the shoulders, arms, and hands. She wore a dress with a tight-fitting bodice and wide, flounced skirt. Usually she wore a shawl around her shoulders, dangling earrings, and a flower or fancy comb in her hair. In contrast, the male flamenco dancer danced from the waist down. He held his chest out, his weight over his feet. He created a strong pattern of rhythms called *zapateado* with his feet.

Carmen danced her traditional solo, an *alegrías*, in the male costume of tight-fitting pants, shirt, and short jacket, and she used the fast footwork that was usually done only by men. Although she wasn't the first woman to do so, she was the most memorable. More than once, the power of her steps broke through the floor! Along with her footwork solos, Carmen made multiple fast turns that would stop so suddenly it would take your breath away. All this was done by a woman who was less than five feet (1.5 m) tall and who only weighed about ninety pounds (40.8 kg).

But Carmen didn't limit herself to male costumes or techniques. When she tossed her long, black hair and put on bright, colorful dresses, she showed that she could dance the female dances superbly, too. In fact, she eventually lengthened the train of her costumes to fifteen feet (4.5 m)— three times her height! When she wrapped the dress slowly around herself and then kicked it out so it unwound in midair, audiences rose to their feet, applauding wildly.

Carmen eventually performed with other flamenco artists in various cities in Spain. Although she began to make more money, she never forgot how poor she had been. She was always generous with her family and fellow performers. After each show, Carmen counted all the money that had been taken in. Then she gave each person in the group an equal share of the money. If a couple had a child, they would also receive a share for their child. Even though Carmen was the star, she took the same share as everyone else.

In the 1940s Carmen went to Hollywood and danced in her first movie, *Panama Hattie.*

In 1936, Carmen was performing in Valladolid, Spain, when civil war broke out. Most of her family was still in Madrid, but she escaped by boat to Portugal with her father and her brother Paco. They soon got a contract to perform in Buenos Aires, Argentina, for four weeks. The rest of the family followed as quickly as they could, for conditions in Madrid were horrendous: people were dying of disease and starvation. Sabicas, the world-class guitarist who would become Carmen's companion and principal collaborator, also arrived in Argentina in 1936.

For the next eleven years, Carmen and her large troupe toured South American countries such as Uruguay, Brazil, Chile, Colombia, and Venezuela. Their audiences were wildly enthusiastic and begged them to come back again.

One member of the company recalled, "All forty of us Gypsies went together everywhere. Sadness didn't exist for us. After doing three theater shows we continued the 'fiesta' amongst ourselves. We didn't stop singing and dancing throughout the trip."

Carmen Amaya performing the flamenco in 1941

But the realities of touring were not quite so delightful. There were often arguments between the members of the troupe, between sisters and brothers, or among husbands, wives, and lovers. Sometimes one or more members would refuse or be unable to perform. Many of them were hangers-on, not flamenco artists at all.

As was the custom in Gypsy families, the father was in charge. Carmen treated her father with great respect. El Chino now handled all the money and made all the arrangements, so Carmen had no idea of what was earned or what was spent. She was generous to a fault and not at all concerned with material possessions.

However, Carmen had more freedom and independence than her sisters. She made many of the artistic decisions and, during the performance itself, she improvised and the other performers had to follow her lead. She also had the freedom to go out with new friends—Hollywood star Lana Turner, for instance.

Wherever Carmen performed, audiences raved about her dancing, even if critics sometimes said her dancing was "wild" and not "art." In January 1941, the impresario Sol Hurok arranged her first performance in New York City. She debuted at a club called the Beachcomber. Lola Montes, a young dancer, at the time, recalled: "There was quite a lot of Spanish dancing in the New York of 1941, but the city had never seen anything like the dancing of Carmen Amaya." Within three weeks, Carmen's show was a hit. Hollywood stars came to see it, and people lined up for hours so they could get in.

Carmen was becoming famous. She performed for Franklin D. Roosevelt, the president of the United States, and for Winston Churchill, the prime minister of England. In January 1942, she debuted at New York City's prestigious Carnegie Hall. The little girl who had performed for coins in Barcelona taverns was now making lots of money, and spending it just as rapidly. Carmen spent some of the money on extravagant purchases like furs and jewels; she gave away the rest of it to friends and family.

Although Carmen was making a lot of money, she began to feel insecure about her lack of education. Dancing professionally during her childhood years had left little time for formal schooling. Over the next year, she learned English quickly and practiced her writing. Although Carmen was gaining fame and fortune, for the rest of her life she tried to "polish" herself and develop other skills besides dance.

For years, Carmen and her company toured the United States, South America, and Europe. Touring was a hard life and took its toll on everyone. There were stories that the company existed mostly on hard-boiled eggs, coffee, and chocolate. In 1942, Carmen and the company went to Hollywood, where she danced in her first movie, *Panama Hattie*. She also met other stars like Katherine Dunham, Rita Hayworth, and Mickey Rooney.

By then, the United States had entered World War II. Carmen performed in a number of benefits to raise money for the war effort. She also continued to perform in cabarets, clubs, and luxury hotels such as the Plaza Hotel in New York City.

In 1945, Carmen and the company went to Mexico City. Around that time, Sabicas left the company. He and Carmen had been involved romantically and professionally for eight years. Now their relationship was over, and Carmen was heartbroken. The company continued on to Buenos Aires, which they made their base for the next two years. There Carmen suffered another devastating blow. Her father, El Chino, died from cancer of the throat.

In 1947, when Carmen was thirty-four years old, she returned to Spain. The civil war was over, as was World War II. Carmen must have felt deeply moved, returning to her homeland after so many years. She was hailed by audiences and critics alike. She was so popular that she performed in Madrid for sixty days!

The next year, Carmen met a non-Gypsy from an aristocratic family, Juan Antonio Agüero. He joined the company as a guitarist and soon the two were a couple. All this time, Carmen's family accompanied her on tour. Although there were sometimes arguments and conflicts among the members, they stayed together and helped each other for many years. Carmen was happy to have the love and support of her family.

In 1951, Carmen and Juan Antonio were married. Now that Carmen's father was dead, Carmen looked to her husband for guidance. Juan Antonio eventually dismissed most of Carmen's family from the company, or they left voluntarily. He began to put her financial affairs in order. At last, Carmen began to have some financial stability in her life.

When she was forty-two years old, Carmen returned to the United States after an absence of ten years. This time, the critics praised her improved technique and maturity. The audiences loved her, too. Domingo Alvarado, one of the members of her company, said, "Carmen's personality was overwhelming, and I have seen people arrive at the dressing room to embrace her, crying … the show tore people apart, whether they liked dance or not. It was as if they had seen something supernatural."

But the frenetic pace of Carmen's life could not continue. When she was forty-nine years old and making the film *La Historia de los Tarantos*, she fainted on the set. The doctors discovered that Carmen's liver was the size of a child's. Her dancing had helped keep her alive all these years, but now it threatened her health. But Carmen declared that even if she couldn't dance anymore, she would still go on stage as long as she was able. She would play the *palmas* (handclap) or sing or do whatever she could.

It was not to be. Shortly after her fiftieth birthday, on November 19, 1963, Carmen Amaya died. She was at her home in Bagur, near Barcelona, her family beside her. More than two thousand people attended her funeral. Carmen is reported to have said, "I want a white tomb with nothing on it, as the tomb of a Gypsy should be."

It wasn't only because of her innovations in flamenco dance that we remember Carmen Amaya. She was a charming, witty, generous human being. For most of her life, she supported her family. Carmen also gave benefit concerts to charities around the world, paying her company's expenses out of her own pocket. She gave money to establish a school for children in her old neighborhood of Somorrostro. The community was so grateful that it erected a monument and a fountain in her honor.

During the 1930s, '40s, and '50s, Carmen Amaya brought flamenco to a popularity it had not known before. She left a permanent impression on her contemporaries as well as on dancers who followed after her. Carmen Amaya was the queen of flamenco.

Pearl Primus

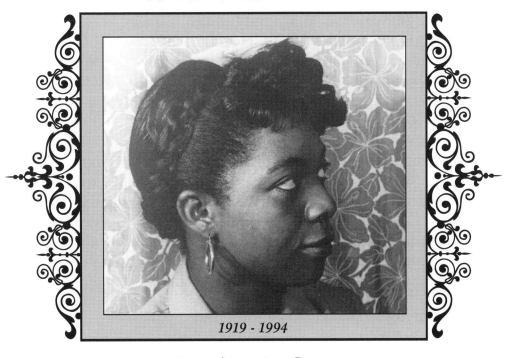

1919 - 1994

Searching for Roots

When Pearl Primus was researching dance in Africa, before she arrived at a new village, the "talking drums" announced that she was coming. They beat out the message, "Little Fast Feet is on her way."

During her long career as a performer, choreographer, and teacher, Pearl created riveting dance works about the cultures of Africa and the injustices in American society. She helped African Americans feel proud of their heritage. She influenced generations of African-American dancers and choreographers—Alvin Ailey, Donald McKayle, and Jawole Willa Jo Zollar, for example.

Pearl was born on November 29, 1919, in Port-of-Spain on

the island of Trinidad, in what was then called the British West Indies. Her parents, Emily and Edward, immigrated to New York City when Pearl was two years old. Emily was tall, lovely, and an excellent dancer. Edward was a capable, hard-working man. Dance was important in Pearl's family. Her grandfather had been a respected dancer, and her mother taught her many of the dances of Trinidad.

In an early interview, Pearl said that she was raised "in a narrow circle that embraced church, school, library, and home." She felt lucky that the racial prejudice about which she later made dances didn't affect her during her childhood. When she was a child, Pearl became fascinated by Africa. She recalled, "I grew up in a home where discussions about Africa were everyday occurrences. My father and uncles had been in various countries in Africa, either as merchant seamen or as soldiers." She promised herself that some day she would travel to Africa.

Pearl was an excellent student and a talented athlete. She loved track and field, tennis, badminton, and hockey. Her strength and speed would show up later in her powerful dance performances.

After high school, Pearl attended Hunter College. In 1940 she earned her bachelor's degree in biology and pre-medical sciences. Pearl had reached a turning point in her life. She wanted to become a doctor, but she needed to earn money to pay for medical school. She applied for a job as a laboratory technician, but because of racism, no jobs like that were open to African Americans.

Pearl tried to get all kinds of jobs, but she kept getting turned away. In 1941, she finally found a job with the federal government. She worked in the wardrobe department in the theater division of the National Youth Administration (NYA), an agency which gave jobs to young people.

An adviser at the NYA suggested that Pearl become an

understudy for a stage show called America Dances. When one of the dancers didn't show up for a performance, Pearl found herself on stage. The audience applauded her loudly. But Pearl wasn't ready to give up her dream of becoming a doctor.

For a while, Pearl studied health education at New York University, but then she went back to Hunter College to work on a master's degree in psychology. However, she felt she was getting too emotionally involved in the cases she had to study. So Pearl transferred again—this time to Columbia University, where she began to study anthropology.

All the while, Pearl was becoming more involved in dance. In 1941, she heard about auditions for the New Dance Group. The company and school had been founded in 1932 to "make dance a viable weapon for the struggles of the working class." The New Dance Group made a point of including everyone— no matter what their race or religion. Pearl got a work-study scholarship at the school.

For every hour of work she did, she was allowed one hour of dance lessons. The work wasn't easy. Pearl had to wash floors, clean toilets, and take out the garbage. But she was determined to succeed. In order to earn money, she took other jobs, too—photographer's model, switchboard (telephone) operator, and welder in a factory.

When Pearl went to her first modern dance class, someone told her that she should warm up. But Pearl was so inexperienced that she didn't understand what that meant. She said, "What do you mean warm up? I'm warm already."

Pearl began to study dance in earnest. She took classes with fellow Trinidadian Belle Rosette, a specialist in Caribbean dance, as well as with modern dancers Jane Dudley, Sophie Maslow, and William Bales. She also studied with modern dance pioneers Martha Graham, Hanya Holm, Doris Humphrey, and Charles Weidman. Years later, she recalled the rigorous training: "My insides thoroughly enjoyed it."

Martha Graham called Pearl a "panther"; Charles Weidman, his "little primitive." Although in hindsight we might call such terms racist, these leaders of modern dance certainly admired Pearl for her strength, speed, power, and talent. She was their only black student.

The 1940s and '50s were a time of segregation and discrimination, a time when it was difficult for an African American to gain recognition in the modern dance world, which was dominated by white people. African Americans who went to dance concerts had to enter through the side door or back door; they had to sit in the balcony apart from white people. In a very real sense, African Americans who wanted to have a dance career had to push their way through the back door.

Pearl's first professional performance took place on February 14, 1943, at the 92nd Street YMHA—known as the "Y"—in New York City. She appeared in a program called "Five Dancers." It was a stunning debut. Several of her works that night have become modern dance classics: *Strange Fruit, Hard Times Blues*, and *African Ceremonial*.

Strange Fruit tells the story of a lynching from the unusual perspective of a white woman. The dance begins after the mob has hanged a man. The body hanging from the tree is the "strange fruit." People marveled at Pearl's expressive choreography—the way she clasped her hands, twisted her arms above her head, and contracted her belly as if she were in great pain.

Pearl wondered how the audience would react to *Strange Fruit*. Would they understand the message? She said, "I want my dance to be a part of the conscience of America." She accomplished this goal. People were profoundly moved after seeing her work, and many cried.

African Ceremonial was a dance based on a fertility rite of the Belgian Congo (now called the Democratic Republic of the Congo). To prepare, Pearl read books, looked at photographs, and visited museums. She asked African students at Columbia University to check if her movements were authentic. She sought advice from two expert percussionists.

After the concert, John Martin, a prominent New York dance critic, wrote: "If Miss Primus walked away with the lion's share of the honors, it was partly because her material was more theatrically effective, but also partly because she is a remarkably gifted artist." In fact, John Martin encouraged Pearl to make dance her career.

In 1944, Pearl worked as a cotton picker in the southern US so she could learn about the oppression, fear, and degrading conditions that were the result of racial prejudice. She worked these real life experiences into her choreography.

African-American dancers at that time often had difficulty finding stages where they were allowed to perform; in order to make a living, they sometimes had to perform in unusual venues. In April 1943, Pearl approached the manager of Café Society Downtown, an integrated Greenwich Village jazz club. He took one glance at this young woman in her pleated skirt, and was ready to send her away. But then Pearl showed him the glowing reviews from the Y concert. He decided to try her out for ten days. The run lasted for ten months.

Every night, Pearl performed two or three fifteen-minute shows. They included different styles—African, modern, and jazz. Audiences and critics alike raved about her talent, her sincerity, and her beauty. Dance critic Edwin Denby wrote: "The leaps can be thrilling, the quickness of the feet a delight."

In the 1940s, people in the United States were beginning to wake up to the deep divisions within their society. During the war years (1941–1945), although about one million African Americans served in the armed forces, the military was segregated into separate black and white units. African Americans talked about a "Double V" victory—over the enemy abroad and over the enemy (racism, discrimination, and prejudice) at home.

At Café Society, Pearl met a group of politically active African-American singers and entertainers, including Lena Horne, Billie Holiday, and Paul Robeson. Through their influence and support, Pearl began to participate in the Negro Freedom Rallies during the war years. Sponsored by the Negro Labor Victory Committee, these rallies encouraged people to work for their democratic rights at home as well as overseas.

In June 1944, the program of the Negro Freedom Rally at Madison Square Garden included a pageant called "New World A-Coming." Well-known black artists and leaders took part. Pearl danced, Paul Robeson sang, and Adam Clayton Powell, Jr. delivered a political speech.

During this period of her career, most of Pearl's dance themes were about African Americans. For example, in 1943 she choreographed *The Negro Speaks of Rivers* to a poem by Langston Hughes. The dance showed the history of slave labor from the pyramids of Egypt to the plantations of America. The critic Margaret Lloyd called the piece "beautiful with undulating rhythms over deep-flowing currents of movement that wind into whirlwind spins."

Despite her success, Pearl began to feel that something was missing. She wondered if her work was authentic. She wanted to "know my own people where they are suffering most." In the summer of 1944, she traveled to the southern states of Georgia, Alabama, and South Carolina. She pretended she was a migrant worker and did the backbreaking work of picking cotton in the fields.

She learned firsthand about the oppression, fear, and degradation that resulted from racial prejudice. In dozens of small churches, she also found rhythms, songs, and movements like those from Africa. She felt she was getting closer to what was real, something that couldn't be learned from books. Pearl wrote down her experiences in diaries and notebooks. The material she gathered became the basis for her pieces *Steal Away to Freedom* and *Slave Market*.

When Pearl came back to New York, she continued to choreograph and perform. She debuted on Broadway on October 4, 1944, where she performed solo pieces and choreographed *Ague* (a work for four men), *Slave Market,* and *Mischievous Interlude.* In an interview a few months after she returned from the South, she said: "I see ... an Africa of nations, dynasties, cultures, languages, great migrations, powerful movements, slavery ... all that makes life itself. This strength, this past, I try to get into my dances."

In December 1944, Pearl gave a concert at the Roxy Theater. She re-choreographed *African Ceremonial*, this time for a group of fourteen dancers. In January 1945, she collaborated with several other artists in a multi-ethnic concert called India-Haiti-Africa. In February, she appeared with her former teacher, Charles Weidman, in a joint concert.

The next few years were filled with new and exciting projects. In 1945, Pearl appeared on Broadway in a revival of the musical *Showboat.* She was a featured soloist in two numbers: "No Shoes" and "Dance of the Dahomeys." The show ran for most of the year and then went on tour.

Pearl wanted to continue her concerts, so she left *Showboat.* Beginning in November 1946, she went on a tour that took her all over the United States. She and two other dancers performed in several new dances Pearl had created, including *Myth* and *To One Dead.*

After the tour was over, Ruth Page, ballet director of the Chicago Civic Opera, invited Pearl to dance in a 1947 revival of the opera *The Emperor Jones.* In early August of that year, Pearl also danced at the Jacob's Pillow Dance Festival where she presented several new works: an Afro-Cuban work titled

Santos and two spirituals—*Goin' to Tell God All My Troubles* and *In That Great Gettin'-Up Mornin'.* In December, Pearl choreographed dances and performed in a short-lived Broadway show called *Caribbean Carnival.*

Pearl could have continued in this way, dividing her time between Broadway and the concert stage, but a surprising event happened in April 1948 that led her to the next stage of her career.

Months earlier, Pearl had applied for a grant from the Rosenwald Foundation. She had asked for money to keep her small company together and give her the breathing space she

Pearl Primus in *Strange Fruit* (1951)

needed to create new works. She had been turned down. After years of philanthropic work, the Foundation was winding down its activities and was no longer giving money to artists and non-profit organizations.

But one evening after seeing Pearl perform, Dr. Edwin Embree, president of the Rosenwald Foundation, asked Pearl when she had last traveled to Africa. Pearl replied that she had never been there. Edwin was so amazed that he arranged for the Foundation to give Pearl its last (and largest) grant. The money would enable her to study and live in Africa for nine months. Pearl's childhood dream was about to come true.

In December 1948, Pearl began her journey to Africa. She was twenty-nine years old, a young black woman traveling all alone to do dance research in such countries as Ghana, Senegal, and Liberia. The story goes that she carried a gun and a can of insecticide with her for protection.

Wherever she went, Pearl lived among the local people, sharing their daily lives and learning their languages. She studied the dances of more than thirty different groups of people. She took photos, made short movies, and drew pictures. She filled numerous notebooks and diaries with her observations. When she was allowed, she also participated in the people's dances.

Pearl was welcomed by the African people. They were amazed that her dancing and their own had so many similarities. They hailed her as a long-lost relative. In Nigeria, she was called "Omowale," which means "child has returned home."

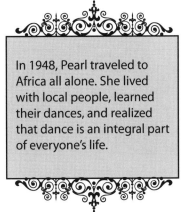

In 1948, Pearl traveled to Africa all alone. She lived with local people, learned their dances, and realized that dance is an integral part of everyone's life.

Pearl learned a lot during her time in Africa. She discovered the tremendous variety of movement in

African dance; that there was no one particular "African" dance style or technique. She realized that dance is an integral part of all people's lives; that there is, in her words, "a strange but hypnotic marriage between life and dance."

When Pearl came back to the United States, she changed the focus of her career. She wanted to share what she had learned, so she began to teach and give lecture-demonstrations more frequently. For example, she used a small group of performers to present Caribbean and African dances in various venues; she gave talks about African culture; and she spoke about Africans who had been forced into slavery.

Pearl continued to give dance concerts. She used a group of male dancers to capture the strength and vitality of the men's dances she had seen in Africa. She created new works like *Fanga*, based on a welcome dance in Liberia. She began to combine individual dances into larger works, such as *Excerpts from an African Journey*.

In 1951, Pearl began to tour outside the United States. She performed in England, France, Italy, and Finland. In 1952, she toured Israel, where she and her company danced in theaters, settlements, and immigration camps. All the while, she was creating new dance works: *Impinyuze*, based on a dance from the Belgian Congo, and *Dance of Strength*, based on a dance from Sierra Leone.

Pearl also continued to do anthropological research. In the summer of 1953, she went to the West Indies. While she was in Trinidad, she visited her former teacher, Belle Rosette. Even more important for Pearl personally, she met Percival Borde, a handsome dancer, choreographer, and teacher whom she married the following year. In 1955, their son, Onwin, was born. He later became a dancer, musician, and stage manager.

Pearl spent the late 1950s giving solo concerts, dancing with Percival in their dance company (now called the Primus-Borde Company) and working toward a PhD in anthropology.

In 1959, the government of Liberia asked Pearl and Percival to establish the African Arts Center in their capital city of Monrovia. For two years, they collected and recorded dances, taught classes, and organized professional performances. They also tried to create audiences for these performances. Unfortunately, the money ran out before they finished their work.

When the couple returned to New York, they opened the Primus-Borde School of Primal Dance. In addition to teaching in her own studio, in 1966 Pearl began a program called "Meet Africa." She wanted to introduce elementary school children to the music, dances, and cultures of Africa. She knew how important it was to convey the depth and breadth of African cultures to her own generation and to generations to come.

In 1977, Pearl earned her PhD in educational sociology and anthropology. Although she continued to dance until 1981, she concentrated on teaching and choreographing. She taught ethnic studies at the Five Colleges, a group of postsecondary institutions in Massachusetts—Amherst, Smith, Hampshire, and Mount Holyoke colleges, and the University of Massachusetts—and dance education at New York University.

Pearl and Percival collaborated on a concert of African, Caribbean, and Afro-American dances which they called *Earth Theater*. They presented the works in theaters and churches in New York City. In addition, they opened the Pearl Primus Dance Language Institute in their home in New Rochelle, New York.

When Percival died in 1979 at the age of fifty-six, it was a huge blow to Pearl. Not only had they been a loving couple, but they had worked together for years. Percival had been respected by everyone both as a person and as a performer. Now, at the age of sixty, Pearl was a widow and on her own. She was determined more than ever to keep working.

Pearl's creations began to be recognized by dance companies. In 1974, the Alvin Ailey American Dance Theater reconstructed *The Wedding*, one of Pearl's works from the early 1960s. In 1990, the same theater revived *Impinyuze*. As she worked with the dancers, Pearl told them: "What I pass on to you is the spirit of the people. I do not want you to let this go." In 1988, *Strange Fruit*, *Hard Times Blues*, and *The Negro Speaks of Rivers* were performed at the American Dance Festival.

Pearl received many awards during her lifetime, including the Liberian Star of Africa (1949), the Alvin Ailey Dance Pioneer Award (1978), and the National Medal of the Arts (1991). On October 29, 1994, Pearl died in New Rochelle, at the age of seventy-four.

Even after her death, Pearl's work continues to inspire. In 2002, the Five Colleges in Massachusetts wanted to honor Pearl. They sponsored a series of events called "Zollar on Primus: Riffing the Legacy." Jawole Willa Jo Zollar's company, Urban Bush Women, performed an original dance suite called *Walking With Pearl*. The dance included "Bushasche," a dance to prevent war that Pearl had learned in the Democratic Republic of the Congo on her first trip to Africa. It was originally performed by warriors who challenged the Evil Spirit of War by trampling it to the ground.

Pearl's main aim in life was to help people better understand each other. She had originally set out to become a doctor, but she found that dance was also a way to heal people. As Pearl explained in 1968: "Because through dance I have experienced the wordless joy of freedom, I seek it more fully now for my people and for all people everywhere."

Alicia Alonso

1921 -

Overcoming All Obstacles

A girl who wants to become a dancer often has many obstacles to overcome—and Alicia Alonso had problems that would have made the bravest would-be dancer give up in despair. Alicia became one of the greatest ballerinas in the world, but for most of her life she was blind.

Alicia was born on December 21, 1921, in Havana, Cuba—only a few years after Anna Pavlova had performed there. She was the youngest child of Antonio Martinez, an army veterinary surgeon, and Ernestina, a homemaker. Alicia's family nicknamed her Unga, which means "Hungarian" in Spanish. They thought she looked like a Gypsy, with her dark skin, black hair, and large, shining eyes.

From an early age, Alicia loved to listen to music for hours at a time while she danced with a blanket or a scarf. Alicia recalled, "Every time I listened to music, I needed to express myself with it, to dance to that music, to move with it." When Alicia was nine years old, she began ballet classes with Nikolai Yavorsky, a Russian man who was the first ballet teacher in Cuba.

After only one year of classes, Alicia performed in public for the first time in *The Sleeping Beauty.* She dreamed of becoming a professional dancer—a career that her middle-class parents considered coarse and vulgar. The only career they wanted for their daughter was marriage. Alicia managed to fulfill both her own and her parents' dreams.

In 1937, the fifteen-year-old fell in love with a fellow dance student, Fernando Alonso and married him. (In those days, it was not uncommon for a Cuban girl of Alicia's age to get married.) They soon moved to New York City, where they stayed with relatives. The next year, they had a daughter whom they named Laura. Eventually, they had to send Laura back to Cuba to be raised by Alicia's parents. Alicia knew she couldn't take care of a baby while she was trying to advance her career.

Alicia and Fernando hoped to launch their professional careers in the big city, but life was hard. They were very poor and Alicia could barely speak English. In order to earn money, she worked on Broadway as a "hoofer," a dancer in the chorus line, in two musicals: *Great Lady* in 1938 and *Stars in Your Eyes* in 1939.

But dancing in musicals was not what she had dreamed about when she was a young girl. Alicia

As a small child, Alicia loved music. "Every time I listened to music, I needed ... to dance to that music, to move with it."

wanted to be a ballet dancer. Nothing else would do. She managed to continue her training, this time at the School of American Ballet. She also took private classes with some of the best teachers of the time: Leon Fokine, Alexandra Fedorova, Enrico Zanfretta, and Anatole Vilzak.

In 1939, Alicia danced with the American Ballet Caravan, forerunner of the New York City Ballet, under the direction of George Balanchine. Only one year later, she joined another company—Ballet Theatre (later called American Ballet Theatre, or ABT).

Alicia wasn't satisfied with only one ballet class a day, as strenuous as it was. Every afternoon, she took a second exhausting class with Alexandra Fedorova, a Russian teacher. Then, every night before her performance, she did a warm-up until her practice clothes were drenched with sweat.

Alicia made friends with Agnes de Mille, a leading American choreographer. Agnes criticized her friend for working too hard, but Alicia insisted that she had to keep pushing herself in order to get strong. Her dancer's body became tougher; her feet, stronger and more flexible. Agnes described Alicia like this: "Her nose is straight and large, with the sensitive, quivering nostrils of a doe, alert to any signal. Her neck is long and supple, bearing the elegant little head like a tropical flower on a tender stalk. Her body is small, beautifully formed, with small breasts and hips, long arms and legs, the feet and arches of a great dancer."

Although Alicia's star was rising, in a short time it would crash down to earth. Alicia began bumping into people and furniture, and losing her balance during turns. In 1941, she was diagnosed with a detached retina in her right eye. The retina is a thin membrane of nerve tissue that lines the back of the eye. When the inner layer of the retina separates from the wall of the eye, a person has blurred vision or loss of peripheral (side) vision.

When Alicia lost her sight, audiences didn't know she was almost blind. In fact, an almost-invisible wire was stretched across the edge of the stage at waist height to let her know she was close to falling into the orchestra pit.

Alicia had an operation to correct the problem, but afterwards she had to lie perfectly still in bed for three months so that her eye would heal. Alicia found it impossible to obey the doctors completely. She had to move her feet, pointing and stretching them. She said, "I have to keep my feet alive."

When the bandages finally came off, Alicia was shocked to learn that the operation hadn't been successful. She had a second operation, but that one didn't work either. Alicia would never have peripheral vision again and much of the world would always be out of focus. How would a ballerina who was partially blind be able to dance? How could she see her partner and the other dancers? How could she stop herself from crashing into scenery or props, or know where the stage ended? Alicia had to learn how to cope with all those hazards if she wanted to continue to dance.

Much to her dismay, Alicia soon had to have a third operation. This time, she returned home to Cuba. Her doctors ordered her to lie completely motionless in a dark room with both her eyes bandaged for one whole year. She couldn't play with her little daughter, chew her food hard, laugh or cry, or even move her head. This must have been torture for Alicia, for when she felt angry or sad, she couldn't even cry about it. Fernando stayed with her every day, and they practiced the great dancing roles of classical ballet by using their fingers on top of Alicia's blanket. She later said, "I danced in my mind. Blinded, motionless, flat on my back, I taught myself to dance *Giselle*."

After many months, Alicia was allowed to leave her bed, although the doctors said that dancing was still out of the question. Every day, she walked with her dog to the ballet studio two blocks away. She wanted to dance so much that she began to practice in secret.

Then, just as she was starting to hope that she might dance again, a hurricane shattered a door in her home in Havana. Glass splinters sprayed onto her head and face, and she fell down hard onto the ground. By some miracle, her eyes hadn't been touched. When the doctor saw this, he let Alicia start dancing again. He figured that if she could survive flying glass, torrential rains, and a bad fall, she should be allowed to dance.

In 1943, an impatient Alicia returned to ABT in New York City. It had been almost two years since she had been forced to stop dancing. She needed to rebuild her technique and relearn how to move on the stage. She had only partial sight in one eye and no peripheral vision in the other at all. But she had barely settled in when she was suddenly asked to replace an injured ballerina in ABT's production of *Giselle*.

Giselle is one of the greatest—and most difficult—roles in ballet. First created in 1841, this ballet has two acts. In Act I, the innocent peasant girl, Giselle, learns that Count Albrecht has betrayed her and is engaged to someone else. The heartbroken girl becomes mad and commits suicide. In Act II, Giselle is transported to the land of the Wilis, vengeful spirits of women who died before their wedding day. The Wilis try to drive Albrecht to his death but Giselle saves him. A ballerina must be a wonderful actress and a brilliant technician to pull off this role. Alicia was both. Her performance was a triumph.

A few years later, Alicia became one of the principal dancers in ABT. During her years with the company, she created roles in modern ballets such as Antony Tudor's *Undertow*,

George Balanchine's *Theme and Variations*, and Agnes de Mille's *Fall River Legend.* But the role she came to be most closely identified with was Giselle. In fact, this ballet became her favorite.

The year 1946 was a turning point for Alicia. The great male dancer, Igor Youskevitch, became her partner. During the next fourteen years, they danced together all over the world and worked constantly on their interpretation of *Giselle.* Igor described Alicia as "the greatest Giselle I ever danced with" and recalled "her vitality and lightness ... her physical and spiritual integration with the role."

Igor Youskevitch and Alicia's other partners learned how to help Alicia adapt to her visual impairment. They would always be exactly where she needed them to be and, using their voice and arms, they would guide her from place to place on the stage. The set designers installed strong spotlights in different colors to help show her where she was on stage. In addition, there was a thin wire stretched across the edge of the stage at waist height to let her know when she got too close to the orchestra pit. Few members of the audience knew that this great ballerina was almost blind. Alicia later said, "You would be surprised how much you can receive by listening. Eyes can be a big distraction, and for all some people can see, they go through life without seeing."

Overcoming partial blindness would have been challenge enough for most people. But not Alicia. She explained: "I am a revolutionary. Because to me, the most important thing is the human being. Human beings are more important than my own art, than my own life. My life, my art, would have little value if human beings did not have the right to go to the theater, to have an education, to have a high standard of living, and other fundamental rights."

In 1948, Alicia returned to the place where she had first taken ballet classes as a child. She was determined to establish a ballet company in Cuba so that people everywhere in her country could be inspired and uplifted by the art that she loved. Fittingly enough, she called her company Ballet Alicia Alonso.

It was a family business. Her husband, Fernando, became the general director of the company; his brother, Alberto, became the artistic director. After its debut in Havana, the company traveled to South America. The performances were popular with audiences everywhere, but the financial situation was quite desperate. Alicia was funding the company from her own savings, along with a few donations from wealthy Cuban families and a small subsidy from the Cuban Ministry of Education.

Alicia seemed to be everywhere at once during this hectic time. In addition to dancing and producing versions of *Giselle*, *Pas de Quatre*, *La Fille Mal Gardée*, and *The Sleeping Beauty* for various ballet companies in Europe, Alicia was a guest star every year with the Ballets Russes de Monte Carlo. The pace was absolutely dizzying! She also traveled frequently between New York and Havana. She was looking for the world's best teachers to train her new students as well as earning money to support her ballet company back home.

However, in the mid-1950s, the political situation in Cuba was worsening. The president, Fulgencio Batista, was a dictator determined to stop any opposition to his rule. He considered all artists and intellectuals left-wing sympathizers, and he cut government funding to Alicia's ballet school and company. At a rally attended by thirty thousand people, Alicia announced her opposition to the regime. Batista's government offered her five hundred dollars a month for the rest of her life if she would stop her criticism.

Alicia would not be bribed or intimidated. Even though she had support from many people, she felt the political situation made it impossible for her to work. She closed her school in

1956, packed her bags, and joined the Ballets Russes de Monte Carlo along with her dance partner Igor Youskevitch.

But revolution was in the air. On January 1, 1959, Fidel Castro and his followers overthrew Batista's government. Castro promised to increase funding to the country's cultural programs, including dance. When Alicia heard about these changes, she eagerly returned to Cuba. In March 1959, she received $200,000 to establish a new dance company, the Ballet Nacional de Cuba. What a relief it was to have the guarantee of annual financial support! Alicia's dream of a Cuban ballet school and company could now become a solid reality, and this time she felt more confident about its future.

Alicia soon decided to take ballet to the people of Cuba—to factories, farms, and military bases. She showed slides, gave lecture-demonstrations, and taught her people about ballet. Not only did she inspire young people—both girls and boys—to become dancers, but she generated a new audience for this art.

Alicia was passionate about using ballet to help children. She looked for talented children everywhere—in orphanages, on city streets, in rural areas. The government gave these gifted children a free education in ballet as well as academic subjects; it covered all of their expenses. Some of them, like Jorge Esquivel, grew up to become world-famous dancers.

Alicia's work went beyond helping talented children to get an education. She believed that dance could be used to treat children who are emotionally disturbed. By doing simple movements or acting out stories or singing songs, these children could begin the process of healing. Alicia called this method "psycho-ballet." She looked at it as "both a discipline and a release."

Alicia understood that many roadblocks can stand in the way of someone who wants to dance. Her company, the Ballet Nacional de Cuba, includes people of all races and all body types—a groundbreaking innovation. In 1964, three Cuban dancers who trained at her school won medals at the International Ballet Competition in Varna, Bulgaria. Cuban dancers continue to be admired all over the world for their ability to combine passion and technique in an inimitable way.

By 1972, Alicia's eyesight had become worse. She could see only shadows, and could no longer gauge distance and depth. She had another eye operation, but she couldn't dance for two years afterwards. Most dancers retire long before the age of fifty-one—but not Alicia. She continued to dance for many more years.

Alicia's passionate stance in favor of the Communist government in Cuba got her into trouble with the American government and American audiences. In 1960, they turned their backs on the prima ballerina who had been so popular and who had, in fact, helped to establish American ballet. It wasn't until 1975 that Alicia was allowed to perform in the United States again. At that time, Agnes de Mille wrote: "She was greeted with a roar such as I have only heard in a football stadium. It was topped by the clamor that broke over her at the close of the work. Alicia was back."

In San Diego, one of the dancers who watched Alicia take a ballet class in 1977 described her like this: "She placed an alabaster hand on the dark, sweat-soaked barre and drew herself up—back straight—head up—ready for the day's work to begin. The pianist played. She pointed her toe. Ah, I thought, that is how a pointed toe really should be! The love and toil of fifty years went into that simple movement. The firm curve of the arch of her foot, its grace and fluidity took my breath away. Expressive as a hand, that foot could punctuate the music or caress the floor. The pink satin of her slipper glowed softly and the ribbons sculpted her ankle." Alicia continued to dance well into her seventies—an unheard-of age for a classical ballerina to be dancing.

A career in dance can sometimes be hard on a marriage. Touring and being away from home, financial problems, and injuries all can strain a couple's relationship. Alicia and Fernando divorced in 1974. In the same year, she married Pedro Simón, a Cuban journalist. Alicia's daughter, Laura, was raised by her family in Cuba and became a dancer. She presently coaches younger dancers and assists her mother.

Alicia received many honors in her lifetime, including the Anna Pavlova Award (1966), the Grand Prix de la Ville de Paris (1966 and 1999), and the Dance Magazine Award (1934 and 1958). In June 2002, Alicia was named UNESCO Goodwill Ambassador for her "outstanding contribution to the development, preservation, and popularization of classical dance and for her devotion to the art form through which she has promoted the ideals of UNESCO and the fellowship of the world's peoples and cultures."

Alicia once said, "Dance to me is life itself." With courage and passion, Alicia Alonso overcame her parents' opposition, political unrest, and even blindness in order to follow her heart's desire to become a world-famous ballerina.

Liz Lerman

1947 -

Helping Every Body Dance

When Liz Lerman was young, she wanted to move, no matter where she was. She loved to ride her tricycle around the tall artichoke trees in her backyard or stomp about in the puddles after it rained. When friends of her parents came over for dinner, they often asked her to dance. She remembers twirling and jumping, and falling down and getting up again. But after Liz had studied dance for a few years, she almost gave it up.

Elizabeth Ann Lerman was born in Los Angeles, California, on December 25, 1947, to Anne and Philip Lerman. She has an older brother, Richard, and a younger brother, David. The family moved from Los Angeles to Washington when Liz was five years old.

Liz's parents sent her to an alternative school where she studied social issues such as racism and injustice. She wanted to make her dance meaningful but the "silly steps" and "make believe" of ballet were not satisfying that desire.

Soon afterwards, Liz begged her parents for dance lessons. Her mother found an excellent teacher—Ethel Butler—who had danced with Martha Graham. Liz loved her classes, where the students did exercises, improvised, and moved across the floor. Sometimes, Liz's father would come in at the end of the class and beat the drum!

When Liz was eight years old, the family moved again—this time to Milwaukee, Wisconsin, where her father's family owned a tire business. Although she was sad that she had to leave her cat behind in Washington, Liz looked forward to the move and playing with her cousins in Milwaukee—joining the "Cousins Club," as they liked to call it.

In the 1950s, Milwaukee was a city of neon signs advertising beer—Schlitz, Pabst, and Blatz. To this mostly working-class city settled by Germans and Poles came the Lerman family—educated, Jewish, and liberal.

Philip Lerman had grown up in Milwaukee. He was a tall man, generous and open-hearted. Starting in the 1950s, he worked hard to improve working conditions for people. He demonstrated against the racial segregation that barred African Americans from schools, clubs, hotels, and restaurants.

Liz's mother, Anne, had beautiful blue eyes and was a good listener. She loved music (especially opera) and working in her garden. She was a strong person and always told Liz to stand up for herself, to have high standards in everything she did, and to find her own way in life. Liz says that she was brought up with a blend of "nurture and rigor."

At the supper table, the family talked about all kinds of issues. They talked about how to make things better for people on the margins—African Americans, laborers, and immigrants. Liz's parents also took their children to a wide variety of shows—"highbrow, lowbrow, always with the idea that everyone had something to say, everybody was relevant." These ideals would have an enormous impact on Liz's life and work.

Liz's dance teacher in Milwaukee was Florence West, who had studied with Martha Graham and Ruth Page. Liz recalls, "She believed we should think a lot. She'd read us poetry. She would make us work with texture. She thought nothing of having us paint for a couple of hours on a Saturday." Fortunately for Liz, Florence also insisted that her students study both ballet and modern dance, an unusual approach for that time. Liz said Florence was "the intersection of my parents. Demanding and rigorous in detail like my mother. Broad-minded and a grand mess of ideas like my father."

Liz's family always supported her. In their home, the arts were important. If there was a dance show on TV, her father would yell up the stairs for her to drop everything (including homework) and come watch. It didn't matter what kind of dance it was—ballet or a chorus line—Liz was supposed to watch it. He also encouraged her to read books "about Katherine Dunham, about ballet, about Jewish theater artists, about Native-American ritual—anything that moved, I was expected to respect and appreciate."

When Liz was fourteen, her beloved dance teacher, Florence West, left Milwaukee. It was a devastating blow. Liz found another teacher, but it wasn't the same.

In spite of the support at home and her love of dance, Liz began to have doubts. It was the beginning of what she calls "my time of troubles." Although she dreamed of becoming a ballerina, she gradually realized that the world of classical ballet didn't jibe with the real world struggles for social justice with which her parents were so involved.

In the mornings, Liz went to Freedom School, where she was encouraged to think about social problems—such as segregation, racism, and injustice—and their possible solutions. After school, she traveled to another part of the city where she was learning the Bluebird variation from *The Sleeping Beauty*. Liz struggled to find her place in dance and in the real world at the same time.

Of this experience, Liz wrote: "The trip took only a half hour on the bus, but it might as well have been centuries long. I had no way of understanding the relationship between the subject matter of the dance and the subject matter of my life. I wanted so badly to be able to make the dance matter, but there was no way that my bleeding feet, the silly steps, the make believe of the dance could match the power and urgency of the stories I was learning in Freedom School." One part of her life was filled with dance, the other part with marches and demonstrations against racial segregation in Milwaukee. Liz was miserable. She made the very difficult decision to stop dancing.

After high school and still unsure about what she wanted to do, Liz went to Bennington College in Vermont, where she majored in dance for two years. While she was there, she realized that her style of dance—what she calls her "Midwestern lyrical passion"—didn't suit the abstract modern dance style that was popular then. She said, "If this was dance, then I wasn't it."

So, deciding to take another break from dance, Liz transferred to Brandeis University in Massachusetts. There she studied history and got involved in the anti–Vietnam War movement. But that wasn't right for her either. So again she transferred—this time to the University of Maryland, where she graduated with a degree in dance in 1970.

Liz's first job after getting her degree was to teach history at Sandy Spring Friends School, a Quaker boarding school in Maryland. She taught there from 1970 to 1973. Liz still hadn't decided to make dance her life's work, although it had begun to captivate her again. After her first year at the school, she began to teach dance—even to reluctant male lacrosse players!

Teaching was rewarding, but Liz still wanted more. She decided to go to New York City, the place where many aspiring dancers go for training. She wanted to see if she could make it in the world of dance outside the university.

She studied modern dance, ballet, tap, and acrobatics. She watched a lot of dance performances, but she felt untouched by most of them. She couldn't understand why other dancers weren't interested in talking about how to apply what they were learning to other areas of life. "I was frustrated with the training itself, which to me felt like people said, 'I'm a dancer if I take five technique classes a day,' and it never mattered what the meaning was."

Liz was beginning to ask questions that had been percolating for years: Who gets to do the dancing? For whom are we dancing? Why are we dancing? What are we dancing about?

Liz started to create her own dances. From the time of her first solo, *New York City Winter* (1974), Liz talked while she danced. She talked about herself, about politics, or about history. She talked about everything—from her experiences as a go-go dancer to her fears about the nuclear bomb.

After nine months in New York, Liz realized that she couldn't answer her questions there. She recalls, "It was cold, distant, and boring. The only people who came to performances were other dancers. The more professional I became, the further I felt from what drove me to dance in the first place." She set out to seek answers elsewhere. She returned to Washington to study dance at graduate school. She was now twenty-six years old and had come to a turning point in her life.

Around that time, Anne Lerman was diagnosed with cancer. Liz traveled to Wisconsin and stayed with her mother during her final weeks. They spent hours together, talking about their lives. After Anne passed away in 1975, Liz wanted to create a dance about the stories her mother had told her. "I always imagined older bodies as part of the scene, usually representing long-lost relatives, or I saw pictures of my mother's own body floating Chagall-like through the living room." But a lot of people thought that older people couldn't, and shouldn't, dance.

That prejudice didn't stop Liz. She started to look for older people for her piece. She began to teach one dance class per week at a senior citizens' residence in Washington called the Roosevelt. From those classes, Liz would find the dancers she needed for her work called *Woman of the Clear Vision* (1975). She ended up teaching classes at the Roosevelt for ten years and writing a book about her experiences there.

This approach broke new ground. It was so new, in fact, that Liz had trouble getting people to understand how it fit with the rest of her dancing and choreography. People told her that if she worked as a waitress, they would accept her as an artist, but if she was teaching old people, she couldn't possibly be a "serious" artist. Liz said that those people "never conceived of the possibility that my work at the Roosevelt was also good for me as a person, as a teacher and as an artist—and ultimately not only good for me, but good for the art form of dance as well."

Liz realized that if she couldn't *find* her place in the established dance world, she would have to *make* her own place. In 1976, she established the Dance Exchange (as it was first called) because she wanted to exchange ideas with people through dance. It started as a school, a performing company, and a way to continue work at seniors' residences and the Children's Hospital.

Liz began to look for a way to create dances that weren't defined and confined by the "cement box" way of thinking. Her company is made up of nine to twelve dancers who range in age from their twenties to their seventies. They comprise a variety of ethnic backgrounds, body types, and gender identities.

Working with older people reinforced Liz's vision of dance as part of life for everyone, everywhere. She believes that "participation is the heart of democracy." Dance should include all kinds of people and should happen in many different places—community centers, places of worship, and public spaces.

Liz began to look for ways to involve people who were not professional dancers. She applied for grants and sponsorships. She banged on people's doors and talked to groups to raise money. And she began to include large numbers of people in her creations. Liz said, "I find much inspiration, pleasure, and challenge in my collaboration with company members, other artists and members of community, just as I enjoy the moments of individual creative leaps."

In 1980, Liz choreographed *Fanfare for the Common Man*. An audience of thousands watched as eight hundred people danced on the steps of the Lincoln Memorial in Washington, DC. In 1986, during the centennial celebration of the Statue of Liberty in New York City, Liz created *Still Crossing*, a work using people from the community. One critic described this production as "a series of simple but evocative gestures—pointing skyward, covering the eyes, dropping the hand and looking into the distance. Performed in unison ... the movements were a powerful expression of unifying disparate parts into a whole." In 1991, Liz led a group of people through the lobby, closets, and even the bathrooms of the Kennedy Center in Washington! And always, Liz stayed committed to creating work of the highest artistic standards.

Liz has always done a juggling act between her dance career and her personal life. In 1980, she married storyteller and writer Jon Spelman. They share a common belief in the power of stories and the need for art to engage with the community.

After their daughter, Anna Clare, was born in 1988, Liz began to wonder how she could raise Anna as a Jew in a "mixed marriage." (Jon is an Episcopalian.) When Liz wants to learn about something, she makes a dance. She says, "When I don't know something, I say, OK, I'll make a dance about it and by the time I'm done I'll know at least a little bit about the subject." Liz explored the question of her Jewish identity in *The Good Jew?* (1991). She danced as if she were on trial, asking if she was Jewish enough. The work generated a lot of interest (and controversy) in the Jewish community.

Being a mother has affected Liz profoundly. She says that it's "like having an extra window into the world." Until Anna was about six years old, Liz took her on tour with her. After that, Jon stayed home with Anna while Liz was away. Anna has grown into a talented, caring young woman who is finding her own path in life.

From 1997 to 2002, Liz and her company were involved in a huge work called *The Hallelujah Project*. She took her company to fifteen communities from Deer Isle, Maine, to Los Angeles, California. In each place, she asked people, "What are you in praise of?" The result was a series of performances combining dance, music, and words. Through this challenging, momentous work, Liz found some answers to the questions she had begun to ask so many years ago about the *who, where, what,* and *why* of dance.

Who danced? Professional dancers, rabbis, ministers, school kids, card players, construction workers, and many more. Where did they dance? They danced in theaters, a sculpture garden, and Buddhist temples; they danced near mountains, the desert, and the seaside. Liz realized that "praise can have many makers and many objects."

Liz knows how to meet people on their own turf. For example, in Deer Isle, she talked with people on their front porches, in fishing tackle stores, and in diners. In every place, she listened to their stories and told their stories back to them. "My work is really about people dancing, not dancers dancing," she explains. Over and over again, people insisted that they couldn't dance, but eventually got up and began to dance.

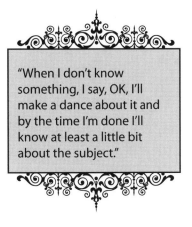

"When I don't know something, I say, OK, I'll make a dance about it and by the time I'm done I'll know at least a little bit about the subject."

In 2005, Harvard Law School asked Liz to create a work to mark the sixtieth anniversary of the Nuremberg trials. During these trials, Nazi war criminals who had committed unspeakable atrocities during World War II were prosecuted.

In this "non-fiction" work, *Small Dances About Big Ideas*, Liz asked what the consequences of evil are and how genocide can be committed even to the present day. Liz calls people who work against evil "upstanders." She believes that through action comes hope. She never forgot the lessons she learned about fighting injustice and apathy when she was younger.

Liz struggled for years while putting her convictions into action, but eventually she began to receive recognition. She has been honored with the American Choreography Award, the American Jewish Congress "Golda" Award, and the National Foundation for Jewish Culture's Achievement Award. Best of all, in 2002 her work was recognized with a MacArthur "genius grant" Fellowship.

When Liz received the $500,000 MacArthur Fellowship, one writer asked her what she would do with the money. She answered, "Part of it is going to be used to send my daughter to college, part to retirement. I'm going to make some donations

The Liz Lerman Dance Exchange company members
rehearse in Portlaoise, Ireland (2008)

Liz leads a workshop on Martin Luther King, Jr. Day
in Providence, Rhode Island (2008)

to the Dance Exchange.... I want to leverage the power of what this means to the world of art."

The Liz Lerman Dance Exchange continues to perform in many different places: seniors' centers, churches, synagogues, schools, prisons, nursing homes, hospitals, concert halls, college campuses, and conferences. By breaking down the barrier between audience and performers, Liz tries to make art matter to everyone.

One of her most recent works is called *Ferocious Beauty: Genome* (2006). For three years, Liz talked to scientists about genetics. She wanted to find visual ways to tell people about the genome, which contains the genetic information, or hereditary material, within an organism.

Here's one way she illustrated this difficult concept: A dancer peeling an apple stands on the stage. The spiral of the peel looks like a DNA chain. On the screen behind her, the dancer's images are multiplied to look like the seeds inside an apple. Interspersed through the movement, we see and hear scientists explain aspects of genetics.

Liz is not only a brilliant choreographer of more than fifty works, but a respected teacher of dance technique, improvisation, and choreography. Her teaching is grounded in her respect for people. She tries to discover each person's point of view and what he or she has to offer. She and members of her company teach in a variety of venues, such as public schools, clinics for HIV-positive adults, and universities.

Liz has developed a way to give positive criticism as she works with other choreographers. She calls this method the "Critical Response Process." Members say something positive about the work; then the artist and the group members trade questions and answers. Group members may express their opinions, with permission of the artist. This process has been adapted to dance, music, and theater departments in colleges and universities throughout the English-speaking world.

Through dance, Liz explores the "juiciness and messiness and loveliness of tearing down artificial walls in order to see what's behind and what's in front of the walls and the people." She continues to ask hard questions and choreograph dances that are personal and political. By so doing, Liz taps into what it means to be part of the human community.

Judith Marcuse

1947 -

Making Connections

*W*hen Judith Marcuse was young, it seemed that she had everything going for her—talent, support from her family, and even some lucky breaks. But over the years, she has faced all kinds of obstacles, including injuries and financial setbacks. Through it all, she has held fast to her dreams until she could make them a reality.

Judith has become a world-famous choreographer, creating dances about political and social issues such as suicide, violence, and the environment. Her work has changed people's lives.

Judith Rose Margolick was born on March 13, 1947, in Montréal, Canada. She is the oldest of four children. Her father, Frank, and her mother, Phyllis, were involved in political issues during the 1950s and '60s. Sometimes they took their children to demonstrations, like peace marches and "ban the bomb" appeals for nuclear disarmament.

The Margolicks' home was filled with music all the time— mostly jazz and classical on the record player. Phyllis was also a talented pianist who played for dance classes in the city. From the time Judith was little, she loved to make up little dances to the music she heard—often by Bach or Mozart. She once created a dance where she pretended she was a milk-maid, balancing a broom on her shoulders like a pole that carries milk pails. Judith also created puppet plays for friends and family who were happy to pay a small admission charge for a worthy cause. She donated the proceeds to the Red Cross and other charities.

Judith's first dance teacher was her aunt, Elsie Salomons. Elsie had studied with Kurt Jooss in London, England, and Anna Sokolow in New York City—two groundbreaking modern dance choreographers. "It was my aunt who started me off when I was three, banging my elbows to the music while my mother played the piano," Judith says.

At the age of fourteen, Judith auditioned for England's Royal Ballet School in an ice hockey rink in Montréal. She studied in London for three years and had a chance to be on the same stage as world famous ballerinas Margot Fonteyn and Lynn Seymour.

Elsie opened a dance studio in Montréal and became a pioneer of contemporary dance in the city. She was a popular teacher and her classes were always filled. She combined modern and classical dance in unique ways. At the end of every class, Elsie would give her students "problem-solving" exercises. For example, she'd describe a word, color, or situation. Then the students would get into little groups and make up a dance about it. Judith recalls that Elsie "believed in the inherent creativity of all of us."

Aunt Elsie wasn't Judith's only teacher. From the age of seven, she also studied classical ballet with Séda Zaré and Sonia Chamberlain. Ballet took hold of the young Judith. She loved its formal beauty, elegance, and discipline. So, when she was fourteen, she auditioned for the Royal Ballet School based in London, England.

The audition was a strange experience. It took place at the old Montréal Forum where fans came to cheer their favorite hockey team, the Montréal Canadiens. The Royal Ballet was going to perform there, so a raised stage had been built over the ice. Three hopeful ballet students walked onto the make-shift stage.

The examiners checked Judith's body to make sure that her spine was straight and that her feet and legs were strong. Then Judith went through a typical ballet class with barre and center work. They must have liked what they saw in this petite, brown-haired, blue-eyed girl. She was accepted. Before she left for London, she was interviewed by a reporter who wrote that Judith "realizes that being a ballet dancer is not an easy life but feels that for her it is the only one possible."

From 1962 to 1965, Judith worked hard, taking classes from several outstanding teachers. One of the exciting aspects of being a student at the Royal Ballet School is that sometimes you're used as an extra in ballets and operas. Judith loved being on the same stage with great dancers such as Margot Fonteyn, Lynn Seymour, and Anthony Dowell.

Though the world of ballet can be very narrow, Judith wasn't isolated from what was going on in the rest of the world. Anywhere she went in London, she could hear music by the Beatles or the Rolling Stones; watch young women dressed in beads and mini-skirts; taste food like Indian curries or Jamaican meat patties. Judith loved going to the British

Museum and the Tate Gallery. She was "sucking it up like a vacuum cleaner."

Near the end of Judith's time at the school, disaster struck. She had just finished a costume fitting at Covent Garden Theatre and was hurrying down the long, circular stairway when she tripped and fell. She landed hard and broke a few of the small bones, called the "metacarpals," in her foot. After taking some time off to recover, she tried to go back to dance classes, but her foot wasn't healing properly.

So Judith had to return home to Montréal. She arrived "crumpled and frightened." Her whole family supported her while she gradually healed. They were good listeners, and Judith was glad that she could talk to them about her fear of never dancing again.

When Judith was ready, she began to take ballet classes again, and was soon invited to join Les Grands Ballets Canadiens in Montréal. During the three years (1965–1968) she danced with the company, she performed in theaters throughout Canada and in forty-eight American states. On one tour alone, she traveled a total of nineteen thousand miles in a bus! Judith described it like this: "There were two buses; the dancers rode in the one with the crummy toilet because the musicians had a union."

When Judith was twenty-two, she realized she needed a change—she was "hungry to explore." For the next six years, she danced with other ballet companies in Switzerland and in Israel. While in Israel, Judith met Richard (Rick) Marcuse, who was working with the oldest modern dance company in Israel—Batsheva Dance Company. They eventually got married and moved to Berkeley, California, where Rick continued to work on his PhD in anthropology.

Judith wanted a break from dance, from the hard grind of the daily routines. But money was tight. To help make ends meet, she worked as a maid in a wealthy household. She even tried selling beauty products door to door. That job lasted for a week.

When Judith read in the local newspaper about a production of *The Nutcracker* by the Oakland Ballet Company, she thought to herself, "Why don't I audition?" She did, and was given the part of Snow.

A few months later, she was asked if she'd like to choreograph a piece for the company. At that time, Judith and Rick were living in the same apartment building as Tim Page, who had been a war photographer in Vietnam. Inspired by the stories he told them, as well as her own anti-war sentiments, Judith created *Fusion* for the Oakland Ballet Company. This piece was about twenty-five minutes long, but Judith never saw the work performed.

In 1974, Rick and Judith suddenly moved to London, where Judith joined the Ballet Rambert (now called the Rambert Dance Company). At the same time, Rick did his anthropological field research about the lives of the dancers in the company. The couple traveled all over the world, as Judith performed with the Ballet Rambert in cities as different as Budapest, Hungary, and Rangoon, Burma.

The Ballet Rambert encouraged its dancers to choreograph new works for the company. Judith's first dances expressed what she thought about and cared about. In 1975, she created *baby*, a ballet about how women can get trapped in roles that men give them. *Four Working Songs*, choreographed in 1976, was a dance about people's working lives.

Judith became known for the way she fused elements of ballet with folk traditions and contemporary dances like jazz, hip-hop, and disco. Max Wyman, a prominent dance critic in Canada, wrote a 1977 review of Judith's dancing. He said: "This is dance to catch and hold the interest, to stir and provoke, dance to lift and excite and elate, dance to communicate." Judith had a lot to communicate. "During that time I

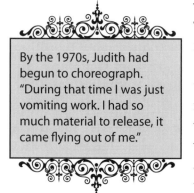

By the 1970s, Judith had begun to choreograph. "During that time I was just vomiting work. I had so much material to release, it came flying out of me."

was just vomiting work," she says. "I had so much material to release, it came flying out of me."

Ballet Rambert offered Judith the chance to create another piece for its next season, but Judith wanted to perform and teach as well as choreograph. There was another reason. Years later, she told a Canadian journalist: "I wanted to follow my own path—it felt like an open field here, where I could just run and trip and fall and not have to pay attention as closely, not have to worry about history." So, after two years with the company, Judith and Rick made the decision to return to Canada.

They decided to settle on the west coast, in Vancouver, British Columbia. It was pretty tough to make a living. Judith taught some classes at Simon Fraser University. She also began to choreograph for ballet and modern companies; for theater, opera, and musical theater; and for film and television.

Starting in 1977, Judith created three or four pieces every year for dance companies all over Canada and abroad. So far, Judith has choreographed more than one hundred original works.

But Judith wasn't content just to make dances for other companies. She wanted to create her own company so that she could work with dancers she knew, build a repertoire at home in Vancouver, and tour beyond the city and the province. So, in 1980, she founded the Repertory Dance Company of Canada. It would change its name several times over the years before settling on its present name—Judith Marcuse Projects. But Judith has always been at the heart of her evolving company.

Judith attracted experienced, committed dancers who wanted to work with her—dancers of all shapes and sizes from diverse training backgrounds— and managed to forge one coherent company. Rick gave up his academic career and for ten years worked as the manager of the company. Judith continued to create new and challenging works, often about social issues. Usually she got rave reviews; other times, lukewarm ones. But she kept making new dances, even though they had to scrimp and save and struggle to stay afloat financially.

The year 1984 was a hectic one. By then, the company was well known and was touring the country. Judith was still dancing, choreographing, and running the company. And that year, she and Rick became parents of a daughter they named Rachel.

Being a mother changed Judith's view of the world. Her priorities shifted and she felt responsible for "this miracle of a child." When Rachel was little, she went on tour with Judith. When she was older and going to school, she stayed home with Rick when Judith was away. Rachel studied modern dance and ballet, and became a wonderful dancer. After high school, she earned a degree in sociology at Montréal's McGill University.

Over the years, Judith's dances have often had social or political significance. But when she was forty-eight years old, she entered a new phase of her creative life. Judith became involved in what would be the first of six annual festivals, called the KISS Festival, on Granville Island in Vancouver. Each year, one special program of eighteen very short new dance and theater pieces were created especially for the Festival. Each of these five-minute pieces had to include a kiss! A lot of the activity was focused around workshops that gave people new experiences in the arts—dance, music, visual arts, and theater. Several productions were presented by youth and for youth.

During one week in the spring of 1995, Judith's company was doing eight shows in a big Vancouver high school. She began to wander around the halls and she listened to what the kids were saying. The atmosphere wasn't anything like what she'd experienced when she was a teenager. She was surprised by the kids' language, their clothes, and how they related to each other. Judith's daughter, Rachel, was about to enter high school. Judith wanted to find out more about what young people were thinking and feeling.

That summer, she gathered together a group of about twenty-eight young people who were willing to participate in games and exercises that contained elements of theater, movement, and mime. David Diamond, the director of a company called Headlines Theatre, also worked intensively with them. The workshops lasted for six days over the space of three weekends.

During these workshops, one issue kept coming up again and again—teen suicide. At the time, Judith wasn't sure what

FIRE... where there's smoke

she was going to do with all the material, but she knew she wanted to explore this painful issue. That first series of workshops led to many more. By the time they were done, Judith and David had involved about four hundred young people, fifteen to eighteen years old, over a period of three years.

Judith took all the material they had gathered together. Along with the playwright John Lazarus and the director Jane Hayman, Judith co-created a new work, which involved dance and theater equally, along with special effects and music. The whole show was based on what teenagers in the workshops thought and felt about suicide. *ICE: beyond cool* debuted in 1997 at the Pacific Centre Mall in Vancouver. Teenagers lined up around the block to see the show; many saw it three, four, or five times; many brought their parents. The play expressed their confusion, anger, and hope.

At every performance, suicide prevention pamphlets written by young people were distributed. At the end of every performance, there were "talk-back" sessions for the youth and their parents. There was plenty to talk about.

The feedback that Judith received was powerful. One young woman wrote: "I chose to take a very large amount of pills of various types and go to bed to never wake up.... I began thinking about the messages that the play was sending out—especially about suicide—and I realized I wasn't ready to go. There really isn't any other way to say this but the play saved my life." The knowledge that she has made a difference to people helps keep Judith going.

In 2000, Judith wanted to take *ICE: beyond cool* on tour, but she needed to raise $1.6 million. She applied for many grants and most of the time got rejections. For one whole year, she kept trying until she finally managed to scrape together the money. This financial crisis was nothing new for Judith. Back in 1984, she had described her struggle to found her new dance company: "This is part of an ongoing battle to convince people that the arts are a completely necessary part of society."

ICE: beyond cool was the first of a three-part project. The next work, finished in 2001, was called *FIRE . . . where there's smoke*. Judith used the same workshop process with four hundred young people, over a period of three years. The piece looked at how youth are affected by violence in their lives— from their peers, from parents, on the street and at home. It's about bullying, racism, abuse, and homophobia. Eventually, this multimedia production was seen on stage and on television by thousands of people.

One teen wrote: "Your play gave me hope, and well, I never thought I'd get my hope back.... I never thought I could be saved, but you did. Who knew that a play could do so much for someone like me?"

The following year, Judith extended herself even further. She became the producer of The EARTH Project. The activities included three years of workshops that involved youth and senior artists in Canada, Japan, and Pakistan. The participants explored issues concerning social justice and the environment.

In 2004, The EARTH Project International Symposium, a UNESCO-designated, five-day gathering of three hundred artists, youth, and activists from twenty-one countries, met at Simon Fraser University in Vancouver. The participants discussed how the arts can be used to create positive change in the world. They also shared their work. Among the keynote speakers were Liz Lerman, Severn Cullis-Suzuki, and Stephen Lewis, former United Nations Special Envoy for HIV/ AIDS in Africa.

One youth delegate wrote: "How has my life been changed? I look at my world through a different lens now. I think about what I'm doing, what I'm buying, what I'm eating. I feel empowered—that my small efforts are in tandem with hundreds and thousands of others around the world. That, somehow, my small actions will create long-term impacts somewhere way down the line."

In June 2006, Judith organized the official festival of the United Nations' World Urban Forum, which was meeting in Vancouver. More than three hundred artists from eighteen countries participated during five days of performances, exhibitions, and workshops. About twenty thousand people came to EARTH: The World Urban Festival.

The third part of Judith's trilogy, *EARTH=home*, premiered at the festival. The piece is about the environment, social justice, and the ways in which we're connected to each other and to our planet. Judith said, "My wish is that we all make art a part of our efforts to create a better, more compassionate world."

As well as producing these huge projects, Judith lectures at universities and conferences in Canada and abroad, including India, Pakistan, Japan, and Holland. She was a board member of the Canadian Conference of the Arts. She mentors up-and-coming choreographers.

In 2007, in a partnership with Simon Fraser University, Judith founded the International Centre of Art for Social Change (ICASC). It's designed to be a global center for networking, learning, and research for people interested in using art to improve society. The Centre helps people from different arts disciplines to work together—writers, directors, dancers, visual and new media artists, and composers. People from many different places, like hospitals, prisons, and governments, are also given the opportunity to collaborate. Judith is convinced that "a lot of the work we need to do has to do with connecting silos."

Judith has received many honors, including Canada's two major choreographic awards: the Chalmers Award in 1976 and the Clifford E. Lee Award in 1979. She is one of only three people who have been given both awards. In 2000, Judith was awarded an honorary doctorate from Simon Fraser University. This honor meant a lot to Judith, since it was a recognition of her work from people outside the dance world. And if you go to Granville Street in downtown Vancouver, you'll see a star with her name on the sidewalk.

The little girl who dreamed of becoming a ballerina has evolved into a dedicated dance artist, committed to fostering all the arts in the world community. In 2008 she said: "I hope that the arts will be seen as a means to clarify, to galvanize, and to empower; that the arts will be understood as essential to us all as we continue to struggle to create a more just and more fully human world."

Jawole Willa Jo Zollar

1950 -

Telling the Stories

When Jawole Willa Jo Zollar began taking dance lessons, she soon realized that her body wasn't made for ballet. She couldn't reach her leg above her head or point her feet like some of the other girls. She felt humiliated when her teacher told her to tuck in her backside. It made her feel that there was something wrong with her body. But that made her angry, too. Jawole knew that somewhere, somehow she would find a way to dance.

Willa Jo Zollar was born on December 21, 1950, in the "inner city" of Kansas City, Missouri. (She would add Jawole to her name later.) She was the third of six children—three girls and three boys.

Jawole's mother, Dorothy, had been a dancer, but she had stopped performing by the time Jawole was born. She told Jawole stories about her life in vaudeville and sometimes she demonstrated movements from her shows. Dorothy was always interested in people, no matter who they were. For example, even though the 1950s were a conservative, straight-laced time, Dorothy accepted a cousin who was gay.

People loved to come to the Zollars' home to sing and play music, or to have a bowl of "gumbo," the delicious soup that Dorothy was famous for. Sometimes Jawole would go to the musicians' union club where people would have jam sessions. At the time, she didn't think there was anything particularly special about this.

Jawole's father, Alfred Jr., had lost his mother when he was three and had been raised mostly by his father. He grew up in poverty and had to work at three jobs during the week so he could go to school. During World War II, he served in the American forces. After the war, he established a successful real estate business and helped found a golf club for black people. (In those days, golf and country clubs didn't admit African Americans and other minorities such as Jewish people.)

Kansas City was segregated. The white people lived in one neighborhood; the black people in another. When Jawole was young, she thought the whole city was black! She grew up immersed in the culture of church picnics, songs, and dances from the African-American tradition. People moved in a funky, swinging kind of style that eventually led to street dance styles like hip-hop.

When Jawole was about seven years old, she and her older sister, Donna, began ballet classes with Tatiana Dokoudovska ("Miss Tania"). They were the only black students in the class. Jawole didn't like the classes with this strict, highly critical teacher.

But Jawole wanted to dance. Her mother found another teacher—Joseph Stevenson, who had been a student of the renowned African-American dancer, Katherine Dunham. His studio was in the heart of the African-American community in Kansas City. He taught his students many dance styles, but not modern or ballet.

Jawole and Donna began to dance in floor shows at parties, and eventually were part of an act that performed in night clubs. Jawole later recalled: "We got twenty-five dollars a show, and that was pretty good for an eight-year-old kid. Also, on top of it, you got money for how you performed during your improvisational solo." She quickly learned that a dancer would be paid for performing and that the better the performance, the more money she got. This lesson would stand her in good stead later.

Joseph encouraged Jawole to develop her own individual style—not to copy someone else, but to do her "own thing." Jawole took this advice, and she and Donna started a small business. They made up dances for people. For example, if they heard someone was having a birthday party, they offered to make up a birthday dance. They'd perform the dance and get paid.

While Jawole was in high school, she danced in talent shows and for a time was on a drill team. But she was a shy, introverted kid. Her favorite activity was to read books of all kinds, even the encyclopedia. One book was a "life-changing experience" for her. It was *Brown Girl, Brownstones* by Paule Marshall. Jawole says it was the first book she ever read that revealed the inner world of an African-American girl's life.

After high school, Jawole went to the University of Missouri in Kansas City to study dance. She later recalled, "I was making dances.... I was part of a black theater group, but I was always engaged in dance and politics and experimentation." There she studied ballet again with Miss Tania, but this time

Jawole appreciated the "discipline of what it meant to be a professional dancer. Not just to feel good, but there was a real commitment to the discipline of it all." In 1975, she received her bachelor of arts in dance.

Jawole next went to Florida State University (FSU) in Tallahassee, where she studied ballet and modern dance. She earned a master of fine arts in dance in 1979; however, that did not satisfy her need to explore who she was as a black woman dancer. She tried to figure out how to translate her life into movement. How could she express the rage and anger, the sadness and bitterness, the joy and humor that came out of the African-American experience?

Around that time, many African Americans were changing their names as a way to get in touch with their heritage. Willa Jo Zollar chose "Jawole" (pronounced Ja-wo-láy), a Yoruba word that at first she thought meant "clear water"; later, she found out that it means "she enters the house." Still, this is a fitting name, for Jawole has entered many different "houses" during her life.

Jawole was feeling tugged in different directions. She had been immersed in African-American dance styles in her community; she had learned the Dunham-influenced technique, with its emphasis on hip movements and isolation of body parts; and she had trained in ballet and modern dance in college. In a 1990 interview in *People* magazine, Jawole said, "What was lacking was who I was. It was someone else's vision."

Then one day at FSU, Jawole watched a performance of a group led by Dianne McIntyre, an experimental black choreographer. Jawole loved the real, gritty work that Dianne was doing. She went right up to Dianne and announced that she wanted to join her company. Instead, based on Jawole's work, Dianne gave her a scholarship to study at Sounds in Motion, her studio in New York City.

In 1980, Jawole moved to New York. She later reflected: "So many people came through Dianne's studio. If you didn't feel connected to the downtown scene, which was mostly white but not completely, or if you weren't drawn to the [Alvin] ˙iley scene, which was powerful and beautiful but which wa ˌı't where my heart lay, then Dianne was the other hub.... Dianne's vision was singular and groundbreaking."

Jawole studied with Dianne for about three and a half years, but she gradually realized that she wanted to make her own dances, that she had her own voice and her own point of view. In 1984, she founded a dance company called Urban Bush Women, or UBW for short. She said: "I was such an idiosyncratic dancer that I didn't fit anybody else's choreography ... which is probably how I came to look for dancers for my company. The very first troupe was sort of a motley crew, because we were all such highly individual dancers. Most of us didn't fit anything."

The name "Urban Bush Women" packs many meanings. "Bush people" was a term used to describe Africans in a negative way by the white people who colonized Africa in the late 1800s. Jawole transformed that word to mean something positive. For her, "bush" also evoked the inner city, with its power and density. Finally, "bush" refers to the big afro hairstyle that a lot of African Americans wore at that time.

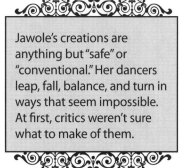

Jawole's creations are anything but "safe" or "conventional." Her dancers leap, fall, balance, and turn in ways that seem impossible. At first, critics weren't sure what to make of them.

It was tough going during those early years. Jawole said, "There's a certain kind of tenaciousness that you have to have when you're thinking of forming a company.... I didn't have a red cent or family to help." Although her family couldn't help her financially, they did give her a lot of emotional support.

During that time, Jawole worked at three jobs and "lived like a pauper to make it work." But she felt that if she invested 100 percent in her passion, it would pay off.

Jawole knew what it felt like to be criticized for her body, so she made sure that no one body type was "ideal" in UBW. The dancers' bodies vary in skin tone (light brown to black), body type (tall to short, thin to curvy), and training (modern, jazz, hip-hop). They come from many parts of the world—Africa, the Caribbean, England, and of course, the United States.

Jawole's dancers all have training in ballet and modern, but they also study other forms of dance, like hip-hop, and they bring their own particular styles with them. Through Jawole's classes and performance pieces, they become stronger and learn to work together and support each other.

Sarah Kaufman, dance critic for *The Washington Post*, described the dancers like this: "None of the eight dancers is like another, yet they share—to an eerie degree—a way of dancing that is like seaweed in a tide pool, fluid and soft but with

Jawole performing with Urban Bush Women

a rock-solid foundation. They gulp space with the overhead swish of a leg or with winging arms. The movement is huge, full-bodied, and effortless."

Jawole works passionately with her company. There is nothing "safe" about her creations. The dancers leap, fall, balance, and turn in ways that sometimes seem impossible. In the middle of set parts of choreography, they improvise movement, always aware of where they and the other dancers are in time and space.

The critics were at first overwhelmed by Jawole's dances. Some writers were puzzled; others were amazed. In a 1998 review in the *Herald Sun*, Kay McLain wrote: "The Urban Bush Women are unabashedly unapologetic about what they are: fierce, feminine, militant, aggressive, sassy, funny, and proud.... This is dance to be experienced, both for its sheer physical force and the obvious dedication of the dancers.... They are synchronized, strong, graceful, and accomplished." UBW has toured all over the United States, as well as throughout Africa, Asia, Australia, Europe, and Latin America.

When Jawole choreographs a new piece, she asks for the total involvement of her dancers. Sometimes it's hard to know who has created what because everyone works together. Having learned from Dianne McIntyre as well as the ensemble theater process of the 1960s and '70s, Jawole once described her method as one that combines "an actor's process with the dancer's physicality." She later explained: "I broke every rule they taught me about composition. I did everything they said you don't do, in terms of making a piece. I was trying to find out, What was my voice? What did I have to say? How could I merge all the things I was interested in into one area?"

Jawole often collaborates with people in different creative disciplines, like theater, art, and music. In 2008, UBW worked together with Compagnie JANT-BI, an all-male dance troupe from the African country of Senegal. Together, they created a full-length piece called *Les écailles de la mémoire* (The scales of memory). Jawole called their work "stunning, powerful, beautiful." One reviewer wrote: "JANT-BI's men and UBW's women are absolutely fierce. They dance with so much intensity that they seem to bounce off each other."

But Jawole and her dancers don't just perform—they also actively engage with the members of the audience. For example, a dancer will call out words and the audience will answer. Or sometimes Jawole will speak directly to the audience, asking them to reply to her questions. At UBW shows, the members of the audience are not passive spectators, but active participants in the creative process.

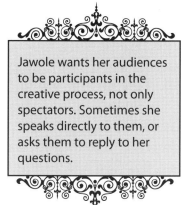

Jawole wants her audiences to be participants in the creative process, not only spectators. Sometimes she speaks directly to them, or asks them to reply to her questions.

Throughout the year, Jawole and UBW give workshops, lecture-demonstrations, and performances for school audiences. Jawole believes that her work as a lecturer and educator is important, but she remains committed to her work as an artist. She says, "Sometimes all the speeches in the world have no effect on people. Art gets to them in another place. There's something very powerful we can do as artists."

Jawole and UBW also get involved in community projects. In 1992, UBW went to New Orleans, where they gave five performances and became involved in more than ten community projects. For example, they worked with teens on a mural filled with social and political commentary, and on a program for the development of math skills through basketball and movement games.

They also do community work at home in Brooklyn, New York. UBW founded and runs a ten-day Summer Institute, and provides partial scholarships to participants who can't afford the tuition. A group of concert professionals and community-based artists attend the Institute in order to "better maximize the possibilities of the arts as a vehicle for social activism and civic engagement." In other words, they brainstorm ways to use art to find solutions to problems in their society and their community. UBW does a lot more. The members of the company present annual workshops, lecture-demonstrations, and performances. One of their projects is to put on what they call "batty parties." In the Caribbean, "batty" (rhymes with "naughty") is a word for buttocks. The members of UBW meet with girls and women to discuss the female body and improvise dances. Then they perform excerpts from Jawole's *Batty Moves*, where the beauty of the female body in all its shapes and forms is celebrated.

BOLD is another initiative of UBW. The letters stand for Builders, Organizers, and Leaders through Dance. This is a program that develops participants' problem-solving, consensus-building and leadership skills through dance training and choreographic development. BOLD is geared to girls and young women, seven to fourteen years old.

Jawole's work has received a lot of recognition. In 1992, she and her company were awarded a New York Dance and Performance Award, called a BESSIE, for their works from *River Songs* (1984) to *Praise House* (1990). In 1998, UBW received one of the first Doris Duke Awards for New Work from the American Dance Festival for *Hands Singing Song*. It was a piece that insisted there was still a lot to be done to get rid of social problems like racism, sexism, homelessness, and disease. In 1994, UBW received the Capezio Award, a ten-thousand-dollar prize for outstanding achievement in dance. In 2006, Jawole received another BESSIE for her work about African-American choreographer Pearl Primus, called *Walking With Pearl ... Southern Diaries*.

Jawole has grown from a little girl who felt bad about her body into an assertive, passionate artist who uses dance, voice, and theater to re-examine history, comment on present-day politics, and struggle against injustice. Jawole said, "I want to create a world in which every little Black girl, every little girl, every child can feel comfortable being himself or herself." Jawole inherited the legacy of African-American choreographers like Katherine Dunham and Pearl Primus, integrated her life experiences into what she learned, and is now expressing her own powerful and defiant vision.

Karen Kain

1951 -

Canadian Girl to International Star

$\mathcal{K}$aren Kain was born in Hamilton, Ontario, on March 28, 1951, into a middle-class family that had nothing to do with dance. Her mother, Winifred, was a homemaker; her father, Charles, an engineer. When Karen was six years old, her mother enrolled her in ballet classes. Winifred thought ballet would help improve Karen's posture. Little did she suspect that Karen would become an international ballet star.

When Karen was eight years old, her parents took her to see *Giselle*, performed by Celia Franca and The National Ballet of Canada. Karen was hooked. Shortly after that performance, Karen wrote: "When I grow up I am going to be a ballerina. I could go out every night and dance. I will be in *Giselle*. It

Karen Kain as a toddler

will be so much fun to be a ballerina."

Karen's first ballet teacher gave classes in a dark, damp basement with a smelly box of kitty litter in the corner. She had only one record—Patti Page singing "The Tennessee Waltz." Listening to it over and over again became a kind of torture for Karen. When that teacher wanted young Karen to go *en pointe*, Winifred whisked her out of the class.

Karen next took lessons from Betty Carey, with whom she studied for eighteen months. Betty was a good teacher and Karen learned the basics of ballet from her. Betty recognized Karen's talent and encouraged her to audition for the National Ballet School in Toronto. In 1962, Karen was accepted. Betty Oliphant, the school's principal, described Karen this way: "She had the feeling which makes people want to watch dancers. She wasn't self-conscious. She had very nice arms and a very good sense of movement. She had the most beautiful style you've ever seen."

The first year at the school was a miserable time for Karen. For one thing, Betty Oliphant singled her out for special attention. The other girls didn't like the fact that Karen was the "teacher's pet." She felt lonely and miserable, and often cried herself to sleep.

Furthermore, the trip back and forth from home to school every day took over an hour each way and she was often exhausted. Even though her parents would have welcomed her back home to a "normal" life, Karen refused to quit. After that year, her parents moved further away, and Karen had to live full-time in the school residence. Gradually, she made friends and got used to the strict routines of school and residence.

Karen was a shy girl who loved animals. Although it was against the rules, she smuggled all kinds of animals into the residence: a squirrel, a pigeon, and even a puppy! She got

Karen at 13 or 14 years old

into a lot of trouble for breaking the rules, but she didn't care. Although Karen often felt moody and depressed during her teenage years, she never let go of her dream to dance.

Karen loved to move to all kinds of music and she loved to jump and run. She has a long neck, well-arched feet, and a high jump. She also has a beautiful face, with well-defined features and large, expressive hazel eyes. But even at the beginning of her training, she had two main problems. By the age of twelve, she had reached her full height of five feet, seven inches (1.7m)—taller than the average ballet dancer. She also struggled to keep her body weight low. She wasn't overweight

Karen Kain in *The Sleeping Beauty* (1972)

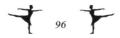

by normal standards, but in the ballet world, dancers are pressured to be below average weight.

Throughout her years at the school, Karen's teachers often said she was "too fat." When she graduated from the school in 1969, she was so worried that she wouldn't make it into The National Ballet of Canada that she ate only salad for two weeks. Of course she was accepted into the corps de ballet, and celebrated by eating a few of her favorite almond cookies.

During her time in the corps, Karen learned how to perform and to work as part of a team. Because of her height, she hadn't had much experience on stage before she joined the company. Karen also learned stagecraft—how to apply makeup and do her hair for different styles of ballet, and even which pointe shoes to wear. (Every ballerina needs to find the shoes that are best suited for her feet. She becomes fiercely loyal to the shoe company, and even to the individual shoemaker.)

Karen quickly moved up the ranks of the company. In 1971, she began what would become a wonderful partnership with Frank Augustyn, another graduate of the National Ballet School. Frank didn't make much of an impression on Karen at first. She said he looked like "a skinny kid with thick glasses, stringy hair, and chipmunk cheeks." And what did Frank think of Karen? She was "just one of the bunheads, her hair pulled back, braces on her buck teeth, small alien ears, and large facial features."

Their partnership was to become famous. In fact, after they won first prize for best *pas de deux* at the Moscow International Ballet Competition in 1973, one critic called them the "Gold-Dust Twins." They danced together in full-length ballets such as *Giselle, Romeo and Juliet,* and *Swan Lake* for about ten years. They had an honesty and directness in their dancing that appealed to audiences. Dance critic John Fraser wrote: "What Karen and Frank offer when they dance together is nothing less than a solemn compact to become one entity."

Karen Kain as Odette/Odile in *Swan Lake* (1980)

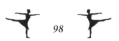

In 1973, Rudolf Nureyev, the famous Russian ballet superstar, picked Karen out of the corps and chose her to dance Princess Aurora to his Prince Florimund in *The Sleeping Beauty*. From 1973 to 1984, Karen danced with Rudolf all over the world, in such places as London, Vienna, and New York. Over the years, Rudolf pushed Karen to develop her technique and artistry.

After her performance of Odette/Odile in *Swan Lake*, a reviewer in Los Angeles wrote: "Miss Kain is undoubtedly a find.... She commands a natural stage personality, sharp theatricality, impeccable musicality, a fine line, astonishing elevation, and an elegant sense of phrase."

Karen was becoming famous in Canada, too. With Frank, she made a television version of *Giselle* in 1976 and of *La Fille Mal Gardée* in 1979. Three documentaries were filmed about her—in 1976, 1989, and 1994.

In 1974 Roland Petit invited Karen to dance with his company in Marseille, France. Roland was a famous choreographer who would create dramatic roles for Karen, such as *Les Intermittences du Coeur, Nana*, and *Carmen*. He said, "Karen Kain is a choreographer's dream. She can do anything you ask her to."

It became harder and harder for Karen to continue her guest appearances with other companies while fulfilling all of her commitments at home with The National Ballet. She was exhausted from the many demands people placed on her, not to speak of the demands she placed on herself. In 1976, she toured Canada with the Ballet de Marseille from east to west, and then went the other way from west to east with The National Ballet of Canada! It took her years to realize that she was trying to please too many people too much of the time.

Karen worked hard to perfect her technique. She once said, "Technique is never something I feel I have the edge on. It always has the edge on me.... It's very strange because I think I was given a gift to dance. I feel music and I have to move to music." Karen always tried to go beyond technique and become an artist.

The downside of being such a perfectionist is that a person can be too hard on herself, and slip into depression. That's what happened to Karen in the late 1970s. She felt exhausted, anxious, and full of guilt. She wanted to sleep all the time, and when she wasn't sleeping, she would burst out crying for no reason. Karen said, "I began to believe that everything I did was no good ... and when you believe that, it starts to get that way.... It was so hard to get myself to go on stage; and when I did, one little thing would go wrong and then I couldn't do anything. It was terrible ... and it just got worse. I no long enjoyed performing. There was no joy in me."

In 1979, Karen decided to stop dancing. She was having panic attacks before going on stage, and felt she was giving terrible performances. She spent a few months in Europe visiting friends, but in the fall she returned to Toronto. At that point, Betty Oliphant stepped in. She told Karen that she was seriously depressed and should get some help.

For the next two years, Karen saw a therapist almost every week. During that time, she faced areas of her life she had never explored before. She learned that she needed to develop interests outside of dance and make more time for friends and family. Karen realized she was no longer a good little girl who should always try to please everyone, but a grown woman who had to take responsibility for her own life. With time, therapy, and her own good common sense, Karen regained her faith in herself and began to love to dance again.

In 1981, Karen broke up with Hollywood actor Lee Majors whom she had been dating off and on for about two years. Soon afterwards, she met her future husband, Canadian actor Ross Petty. After dating for a few months, Karen proposed to Ross. They were married in May 1983.

That same year, Danish ballet superstar Erik Bruhn became the artistic director of The National Ballet. He treated the members of the company like intelligent, creative adults, and he challenged them to be the best they could be. He encouraged them to perform as guest artists with other companies. Karen appeared with Eliot Feld's company in New York City, where he created works especially for her.

At home, Erik Bruhn commissioned new works for the company: Constantin Patsalas' *Oiseaux Exotiques*, Robert Desrosiers' *Blue Snake*, and David Earle's *Realm*. For Karen, the high point was Glen Tetley's *Alice*, created in 1986. It was a powerful new role that allowed her to show her maturity as a dramatic dancer.

In the spring of 1986, Erik became very ill with lung cancer. He died on April 1 at the age of fifty-eight. In a letter to the members of the company, he wrote: "Let's go on from here, spirits up, with confidence, belief, and mutual respect for each other—not only go on, but go on inspiring each other." His death was a huge loss for everyone in the company and for the dance world.

Karen was only thirty-five years old, but she began to think of her future after dance. She got involved in an organization called the Dancer Transition Resource Centre (DTRC). Founded in 1985 by Joysanne Sidimus, this organization helps dancers when they stop dancing. Since boys and girls must start their training at a young age and must dedicate themselves completely to dance, they often don't have training in anything else. When they retire, the change in their lives can be devastating.

The DTRC gives these dancers the help they need to pursue another career. The dancers' interests are quite diverse—one became an organic farmer, another a quilt designer, and another a gourmet chef. Since its founding, the organization has helped more than ten thousand dancers with counseling

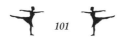

and financial help for retraining. Karen is the president for life of the DTRC.

Karen is not the kind of person who typically goes on protest marches, but in 1995 she felt compelled to express herself in a new way. Along with Rex Harrington, another National Ballet star, and two dancers dressed as *Nutcracker* soldiers, she marched in front of the Ontario Legislature. They brought with them ten thousand signatures protesting budget cuts to the arts. They were called "subversives" and weren't allowed into the building.

Karen laughed about being turned away, but she wasn't laughing about the nearly half a million dollars cut from the dance company's budget. Karen was learning to speak up. She reflected, "All our lives, we dancers have had to deal with the attitude that we're well-meaning and talented children, ill-equipped to do anything but dance. Our fight to be treated as adults with real jobs worthy of respect is just beginning, and the older I get, the more determined I am to make this fight a personal campaign."

Karen in her new role as artistic director of The National Ballet of Canada

After twenty-six years as a principal dancer, Karen gave up dancing full-length classical roles like *Swan Lake* and *The Sleeping Beauty*. But she continued to challenge herself with new roles. Choreographers wanted to create dances for her that would express her artistic maturity. John Neumeier choreographed *Now and Then* for her in 1993; James Kudelka, *The Actress*, in 1994.

Now, as the artistic director of The National Ballet of Canada, Karen says she is like the captain of a ship. Her job is to know everyone in the company and give them the opportunities they deserve.

In 1997, Karen officially retired as prima ballerina of The National Ballet of Canada. However, that was not the end of her connection with the company. After becoming artist-in-residence (1998) and then artistic associate (2000), Karen was appointed artistic director in 2005.

Karen had some real challenges when she took over as director. The company had been losing money as well as audiences over the years. Karen decided to make some drastic changes. She wanted to revive such classics as *Giselle* for new audiences, as well as bring in contemporary, cutting-edge works.

Because Karen had been a dancer with the company for so many years, the other dancers trusted her. They knew she understood their problems. She expected her dancers to work very hard, but at the same time she provided them with more support services, like physiotherapy and massage. She explained: "An artistic director is an ongoing presence that dancers need to feel. Because as a member of a company like this, you want to feel there's a captain of the ship and you want to feel that the captain notices each person in the organization and each artist, and watches their progress, because that person is responsible for giving opportunities.... That's my job."

From 2004 to 2008, Karen was also the chair of the Canada Council for the Arts, the government agency that oversees grants to artists and arts organizations. She wanted to use her celebrity status to remind people that the Canada Council is underfunded and that artists need more support. She felt it was her responsibility to do something for other artists, and to give her time and energy back to her country. Karen pushed the Canadian government hard and, in 2008, she was happy to announce a funding increase of thirty million dollars. Shortly after that announcement, she stepped down as chair of the Canada Council to devote her energies to The National Ballet.

Just as Karen decided to become a ballerina after she saw Celia Franca in *Giselle*, Karen has inspired countless girls to take ballet lessons. One young fan wrote: "I am writing this letter to thank you for a wonderful performance of *Giselle*.... (I don't think you remember me, the little kid with the short blonde hair and gold barret [sic]?) I am a 10-year-old girl who thinks you are fantastic."

When Karen visits the National Ballet School, the young students hover around her like bees around a flower. They ask for her autograph, and, more importantly, her advice. Karen once said, "I have a responsibility that all the young talent that's coming after me has at least the same opportunity that I received, not less."

That shy little girl with the dream of becoming a famous ballerina persevered to achieve her goal. Now, as a mature, confident woman, she is helping others to reach for the stars and realize their potential.

Geeta Chandran

1962 -

Dancing the Old, Creating the New

When Geeta Chandran was five years old, her mother took her to meet the famous dancer Swarna Saraswathy, who was teaching Bharatanatyam, the South Indian classical dance, in Delhi, India. Geeta's mother urged Geeta to offer her future teacher a plate on which were laid betel leaves, a coconut, bananas, and an envelope containing money. Geeta made the traditional bow to her teacher. "And with that act," Geeta later recalled, "not knowing it at all at that time—I was given forever to dance."

Geeta has used the classical dance of Bharatanatyam to talk to people about issues such as women's rights and the environment. By so doing, she has influenced how people view

her dance form, as well as their world. She has evolved from a totally traditional dancer, telling stories about the Hindu deities, to one who tells new stories about contemporary society.

Geeta was born on January 14, 1962, in the city of Cochin, in the state of Kerala in southwest India. She was a long-awaited and much-loved only child. Her father, Ramanathan Ramakrishnan, worked for the Indian government. Her mother, Parvathy, was a homemaker. When Geeta was two years old, the family moved to New Delhi, far away to the north of India.

Geeta's parents loved Carnatic music—the classical music of southern India—as well as Bharatanatyam. Her mother plays the *veena*, a stringed instrument, and is also a good dancer. They often took Geeta to music and dance performances. But Geeta's parents were also quite traditional. School always came first. Her father wanted Geeta to be able to earn a living when she grew up. Her mother was very strict. Geeta had to finish all of her homework before she went to the dance classes she took three times per week after school. There was no television in the house.

Although Geeta didn't especially like elementary school, she was a favorite of her teachers. Her handwriting was the neatest in the class and her projects were detailed and meticulous. Math came easily to her.

When Geeta was eight years old, she began to study South Indian classical music. Early every morning, before going to school, she practiced singing for one hour. Geeta's parents didn't necessarily want her to become a professional musician or dancer, but they did want her to become familiar with her culture and heritage.

Swarna Saraswathy, Geeta's first teacher, was a hard taskmaster. Coming from the *devadasi* (temple dancer) tradition, she had very high standards. Geeta recalls: "You had to conform. There was no creative freedom. Hers was the old-school approach. It was strict and draconian. It also let the art survive without being corrupted. My most valuable training in Bharatanatyam was under Swarna Saraswathy."

"As an artist, my first commitment is to the society in which I live. Its problems are mine.... Classical dance [is] relevant and riveting."

Geeta has many memories of Swarna, whom she calls a "simple, straightforward person." Swarna seldom praised her students, Geeta least of all. Swarna believed Geeta was the kind of person who needed to be pushed rather than praised. Geeta would often run home and cry after her dance lessons, because she couldn't understand why her beloved teacher never gave her a kind word.

Only once did Swarna give Geeta a compliment. During their two-month summer vacation, the students had all forgotten several steps and combinations. Swarna scolded Geeta, "If even *you* can forget, what can I expect from the others?" That small crumb of praise kept Geeta going for a long time.

Swarna taught her students a vast repertoire of dances, but, more importantly, she showed them what it meant to be a complete artist—to dance, sing, play the veena, and conduct. Geeta says that Swarna "had mastered every facet of the art form."

Life was not all work and no play. During the long summer holidays, Geeta went with her mother to stay with her grandparents in Cochin. She played with her cousins—climbing trees, playing games, and making up shows of music and dance every other night for an assorted audience of grandparents, cousins, and servants. In the evening, when her grandmother lit the lamp on her little altar, Geeta felt truly connected to her tradition and her culture.

In 1974, after seven years of intensive dance classes, Geeta had her *arangetram,* or stage debut. She was given the title "Natya Ratna," which indicated that she had completed the first stage of Bharatanatyam training.

After this debut, Geeta continued her dance studies with Swarna. "She made me aware of my spine in both the physical and metaphysical sense.... From Swarna I learned that dance is sacred." In addition, Geeta practiced Carnatic music and learned to play the cymbals.

When she was fourteen years old, the family moved from the neighborhood that Geeta had loved to a more prosperous one on the other side of the city. Geeta went from being the "star" in her old school to feeling like a complete nonentity at her new school. Her grades fell and she stopped taking music lessons. She was miserable. It would take a couple of years before she began to make new friends and feel comfortable at school again.

For a while, Geeta continued dance classes with Swarna. However, it was too far to travel and besides, her teacher was in poor health. It was hard for Geeta to let go of Swarna and find another teacher—especially since all her new teachers were men. "For me, to change from a female teacher to a male teacher was unimaginable," Geeta later recalled. Gradually, she realized that there were other ways to study dance, and that she could learn the new skills she needed from her male teachers.

After high school, Geeta went to Lady Shri Ram College, part of the University of Delhi, where she got her degree in mathematical statistics. While she was there, she met her future husband, Rajiv Chandran. His family was friends with Geeta's family, so the couple had many opportunities to get to know each other. They went to movies and concerts together and found they had a lot in common. They decided to get engaged.

Geeta's father still wanted her to be able to earn a living, so she then went to the Indian Institute of Mass Communication where she got her Master's degree in public relations and journalism. After graduating, she worked as a media researcher for a year. In 1985, Geeta and Rajiv married. A few years later, in 1988, their daughter, Sharanya, was born.

Life seemed to be moving along smoothly, but when Geeta was about twenty-five years old, she realized she could not do justice to two demanding professions at the same time—her

Geeta Chandran, from her book, *So Many Journeys* (2005)

full-time job and dance. She knew she had to make a difficult choice. She went to her dance teacher, K. N. Dakshinamurthi, and asked him if he would train her for five hours a day. He agreed. So Geeta quit her job and began her dance training with a vengeance. She was taking a risk, but it was one she felt she had to take. Rajiv and her parents were very supportive of her decision to devote herself to a career in dance.

K. N. Dakshinamurthi began to work with Geeta, using different body patterns, but ones that were still based on traditional Bharatanatyam. "I had filled myself up with a lot of things," Geeta says, "and he helped me churn all that and try to bring it out in my dance." He also gave her opportunities to teach classes and create new works.

In 1990, after many years of learning and performing, Geeta founded her own school and dance company called Natya Vriksha (The Tree of Dance). She teaches more than eighty students—boys and girls—from the ages of eight to thirty. Most of them are from India, but some have come from other countries, such as Korea, China, France, and Australia.

Teaching has been a great challenge for Geeta. She believes that the process of studying dance enriches her students' lives in many ways. She says, "Teaching has helped me connect with the young minds and help them to understand India better through their dance."

One sign of a school's success occurs when the students reach an advanced level and have their arangetrams. In 1999, two of Geeta's students reached this level of proficiency. Since then, thirty students have had their debuts under her care. After their debuts, students continue studying with Geeta. In addition to Bharatanatyam, they study yoga, music, stagecraft, makeup, philosophy, and mythology.

Geeta and her senior students also visit schools and colleges, where Geeta gives lecture-demonstrations about Bharatanatyam. In this way, she hopes to connect school children to their traditional culture: "We need to invest energies not only in keeping the arts alive, but also in keeping audiences alive. People have to be alerted to the beauty and power of our traditional performing arts."

In March 1999, Geeta performed at the Indira Gandhi National Centre for the Arts to benefit victims of road accidents in Delhi. One month later, she performed a benefit concert to raise funds for the Handicapped Children's Parents' Association. She continues to perform for charities because she believes it is a way she can pay society back for all the blessings she has received.

Geeta's work has had a social impact that goes beyond increasing awareness of an ancient dance form or raising money for charitable causes. In 1998, she was performing in a town in the Rajasthan district. About thirty thousand people were seated around the stage. Geeta performed a dance where an angry Radha, one of the female deities in the Hindu religion, complains about her husband, Krishna, who is seeing other women.

After the performance, a group of young women approached Geeta. One of them started to cry. When Geeta asked her why she was crying, she said that her husband was having an affair with a woman in the village. She didn't know what to do.

Geeta encouraged the women to talk about their problems, to create a support system in their village, and to speak out against all injustices. From that day on, Geeta realized her art could move people to action. "As an artist, my first commitment is to the society in which I live. Its problems are mine.... Classical dance [is] relevant and riveting."

Geeta has continued to use dance as a way to talk about contemporary issues. In November 1998, she participated in a campaign launched by the United Nations Development Fund for Women (UNIFEM). This organization "provides financial and technical assistance to innovative programmes and strategies to foster women's empowerment and gender equality." UNIFEM places the advancement of women's human rights at the center of all its activities.

Natya Vriksha, Geeta's dance company, presented *Sihanvalokan* as part of UNIFEM's Violence Against Women campaign. *Sihanvalokan* was based on an award-winning story by author Asha Bage about women's right to make their own decisions about marriage. It was narrated on stage while the dance illustrated and interpreted the text.

While using the traditional dance form of Bharatanatyam, Geeta has choreographed solo and group works that are relevant to our time. These include: *Pankh* (1995), based on a short story about women's rights; *Sivam* (1999), about the

Geeta Chandran in *Aval* (2001)

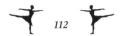

environment; and *Aval* (2001), a group production about gender issues. Geeta does not try to emphasize a message, only to communicate the story in an effective way through dance.

Geeta began to collaborate with other artists. In 2000, an organization called Women in Security, Conflict Management, and Peace (WISCOMP) asked her to create a work about women in war. With her friend, the puppeteer Anurupa Roy, Geeta created *Her Voice*. Together they used their separate art forms—Bharatanatyam and puppetry—to express the horrific theme of women caught in the violence of war. *Her Voice* was performed more than thirty times. Leela Venkataraman wrote in *The Hindu*, India's national newspaper, that the work "was very imaginatively conceived with talents from many disciplines.... The performance came through as a searing plea for sanity in a world dogged by belligerence."

Geeta has collaborated with writers, poets, artists, dancers, and actors. She has used western classical music as well as Indian classical music for her Bharatanatyam interpretations. She has even choreographed pieces to English poetry and short stories. She has also worked in theater, film, and television.

Rajiv helps Geeta with many business matters related to running her school and company, in addition to working as a national information officer for the United Nations Information Centre for India and Bhutan. Geeta says, "My husband has been with me through this journey at every single moment.... It has been a completely shared experience."

> Using her traditional dance form, Geeta has created works that deal with women's rights, the environment, and war and violence. She enjoys finding new audiences for her art form, especially among young people.

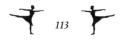

Because Geeta believes that dance should communicate, she enjoys bringing dance to new audiences—children or young adults; environmentalists or business people; tourists or fellow artists. In fact, one of her main goals is to visit schools and teach children about Bharatanatyam.

Geeta is a deeply religious person who observes Hinduism faithfully. Every morning, she wakes up at six to practice yoga, followed by *pranayam* (breathing exercises) and meditation. She likes to walk in her neighborhood, where she can connect to nature. She says her soul is affected by the flowers, trees, colors, birds, and the changing of the seasons.

Geeta feels the presence of God everywhere—in her prayer room, a temple, or in the dance studio. "There, where I create, is also where I encounter God," she says. "In that space, sweat is a ritual, and the body's physical energy is the best offering." Through dance, Geeta tries to find a balance between the calm of her strong religious faith and the turbulence of her fight against social inequalities.

Geeta has received numerous awards for her work. In 2000, WISCOMP gave her a Scholar of Peace Fellowship. In 2001, she was honored with the Dandayudhapani Pillai Award for Bharatanatyam, as well as the Millennium Award from the Millennium Committee for Asia. In 2007, she received the prestigious Padma Shri Award from the president of India.

For more than forty years, Geeta Chandran has studied the ancient art of Bharatanatyam. She has danced the old while creating the new. She explains: "Dance is unique and is a celebration of the highest possibilities of the human body and spirit. Dance refuses to be bound, it refuses to be scared, and it refuses to play by the rules you set it. Dance is the celebration of the individual and of individualism. In a world where similar shades of sameness threaten to obliterate differences, dance proudly says, 'I am free. I am me.'"

Forms of Dance

(From: Debra Craine and Judith Mackrell, *Oxford Dictionary of Dance*. Oxford: Oxford University Press, 2004.)

Ballet: A form of Western dance which began in seventeenth-century France. The delicate and refined Romantic ballet flowered in France in the first half of the nineteenth century with such ballets as *Giselle*. Dance developed a more virtuosic and athletic style in Russia in the latter half of the nineteenth century, the era which gave birth to the three Tchaikovsky ballets (*Swan Lake*, *The Sleeping Beauty*, and *The Nutcracker*). In 1909 Diaghilev brought Russian dance to the West, sparking an international ballet boom that eventually led to the creation of schools and companies throughout Europe and America.

Bharatanatyam: South Indian classical dance. This solo dance form, traditionally performed by women, is over two thousand years old. Bharatanatyam originated in Hindu temples and was performed by temple dancers to tell religious stories and express beliefs about the many Hindu gods and goddesses people worshipped.

Bharatanatyam almost died out while India was under British colonial rule during the nineteenth and into the twentieth century. Only when a group of patriotic people revived it in the mid-1930s was Bharatanatyam performed again in public.

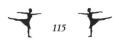

Today, Bharatanatyam has gained new followers and is practiced not only in India but all over the world. Bharatanatyam dancers now perform on stages rather than in temples. Traditional performances can last up to three hours.

The emphasis in the choreography is on the upper body, and the style is distinguished by its low center of gravity, its rhythmic footwork, its straight spine, and its extensive vocabulary of hand gestures which carry dramatic meaning. The face is also used for expressive purposes, with the eyes, nose, and mouth all possessing their specific choreographic language. The dancer wears a silk sari, usually decorated with gold, and her feet are bare, although bells are worn around the ankle.

Flamenco: The traditional Gypsy dance of southern Spain has three main components: It is danced by the body, sung by the voice, and played on the guitar. Before 1782, flamenco was a private affair for family and guests in caves or tents to celebrate weddings, baptisms, and festivals. After that time, when laws against Gypsies were loosened, the "golden age" of flamenco began. In the early 1840s, flamenco was performed in public in small bars and taverns called "cafés cantantes." In this way, flamenco became popular throughout Spain in cities like Barcelona, Madrid, and Seville. Eventually, the cafés cantantes gave way to music-halls and theaters in the cities of Europe and the Americas.

The dance is characterized by supple arm movements and stamping footwork. Individual performances are distinguished by the inventiveness with which dancers play with the rhythms of each dance and by their intensity of expression.

Modern dance: Theatrical dance which is not based on the academic school of classical ballet. Modern dance pioneers rejected the rigid hierarchy of ballet in favor of a freer movement style. Some dancers developed their own technique. Early subject matter was often political or psychological. By the end of the twentieth century, the barriers between ballet and modern dance were less pronounced as dancers and choreographers worked increasingly in both styles.

Glossary

alegrías: one of the flamenco dance forms

arangetram: the stage debut of a Bharatanatyam dancer

bailaora: a flamenco dancer who learns the Gypsy style and technique at home from her family, and who is likely to dance flamenco to celebrate family and social occasions as well as on the stage

barre: the wooden bar attached to the walls of a ballet studio at about waist height. It is used by dancers to aid balance during the exercises that constitute the first part of a daily class

cantaor: a flamenco singer

Carnatic music: classical music of South India

choreographer: the person responsible for creating and arranging the steps and patterns of a dance work

choreography: the art of composing dance

devadasi: a dancer of Bharatanatyam in Hindu temples of India

A dancer's feet
en pointe

en pointe: in ballet, dancing on the tip of the toe, in specially designed pointe shoes that have been stiffened with glue and which allow the ballerina to balance her entire body weight on a tiny flat surface

palmas: the rhythmic hand-clapping which is an essential accompaniment to flamenco dance and often to the song as well

pas de deux: a dance for two, a duet

veena: a stringed instrument used in Indian classical music

zapateado: the rhythmic sounds made by striking the shoe on the floor in various ways; also the name of a flamenco dance

Sources & Resources

* for children

ALICIA ALONSO

Bai, Anjuli. "Alicia Alonso: Partaking of the Magic." *Ballet Magazine* (Dec. 2003): http://www.ballet.co.uk/magazines/yr_03/nov03/ab_working_with_alicia_alonso.html.

De Mille, Agnes. *Portrait Gallery: Artists, Impresarios, Intimates.* Boston: Houghton Mifflin, 1990.

Durbin, Paula. "Legend of Spirit and Style." *Americas* 56 (July/August 2004): 48–53.

Terry, Walter. *Alicia and Her Ballet Nacional de Cuba.* New York: Doubleday, 1981.

Ballet Nacional de Cuba: http://www.balletcuba.cult.cu/Biografias/biografias.html

United Nations Educational, Scientific, and Cultural Organization (UNESCO): www.unesco.org

CARMEN AMAYA

Goldberg, Meira K. "Border Trespasses: The Gypsy Mask and Carmen Amaya's Flamenco Dance." Diss. (D.Ed.). Temple University, 1995.

Pohren, Donn E. *Lives and Legends of Flamenco: A Biographical History.* Madrid: Society of Spanish Studies, 1988.

Queen of the Gypsies: A Portrait of Carmen Amaya. Dir. Jocelyn Ajami. Gypsy Heart Productions, 2002. (Video)

Gypsy Heart: The Heart and Soul of Flamenco / Omayra Amaya. Dir. Jocelyn Ajami. Kultur Video, 1998. (Video)

Flamenco at 5.15. Dir. Cynthia Scott. National Film Board of Canada, 1983. (Video)

"Flamenco—Carmen Amaya": http://www.andalucia.com/flamenco/dancers/carmenamaya.htm

Flamenco World: http://www.flamenco-world.com

GEETA CHANDRAN

Chandran, Geeta, with Rajiv Chandran. *So Many Journeys.* New Delhi: Niyogi Offset, 2005.

Chandran, Geeta. "Beyond Market Forces." *The Financial Express.* 27 Apr. 2008: http://www.financialexpress.com/news/beyond-market-forces/302089/2.

___. Interview with the author, Sept. 2008.

Sawhney, Anubha. "Geeta Chandran: I believe in God." *India Times*: http://spirituality.indiatimes.com/article-show/1544053.cms.

Sethi, Parul. "Dance must be an agent of social change." *The Pioneer.* 9 Aug. 1998.

Geeta Chandran: http://members.tripod.com/GeetaChandran.

KAREN KAIN

Augustyn, Frank, with Barbara Sears. *Dancing from the Heart: A Memoir.* Toronto: McClelland & Stewart, 2000.

Cardinal, Jacqueline, and Laurent Lapierre. "Karen Kain and the National Ballet of Canada." *International Journal of Arts Management* 9.2 (Winter 2007).

Kain, Karen, with Stephen Godfrey and Penelope Reed Doob. *Karen Kain: Movement Never Lies: An Autobiography.* Toronto: McClelland & Stewart, 1994.

* Kaye, Marcia. *Karen Kain.* Markham, ON: Fitzhenry & Whiteside, 1989.

Street, David. *Karen Kain: Lady of Dance.* Text by David Mason. Toronto: McGraw-Hill Ryerson, 1978.

* Zola, Meguido. *Karen Kain: Born to Dance.* Toronto: Grolier, 1983.

Karen Kain: Ballerina. Dir. Philip McPhedran. MasterVision, 1977. (Video)

Making Ballet: Karen Kain and The National Ballet of Canada. Dir. Anthony Azzopardi. VIEW, 1995. (Video)

Canadian Broadcasting Corporation (CBC), "Karen Kain, Prima Ballerina": http://archives.cbc.ca/arts_entertainment/dance/topics/1002/

The Canadian Encyclopedia, "Karen Kain": http://www.the-canadianencyclopedia.com

Library and Archives Canada, "Karen Kain": http://www.collectionscanada.gc.ca/women/002026-603-e.html

The National Ballet of Canada: www.nationalballet.ca

LIZ LERMAN

Borstel, John. "Four Questions, A Thousand Answers." *Hallelujah: The Extraordinary Essence in Ordinary Life.*

Maryland: Liz Lerman Dance Exchange and the Clarice Smith Performing Arts Center, 2002.

Harding, Cathryn. "Liz Lerman: Seeking a Wider Spectrum." *Dance Magazine* (Jan. 1996).

Lerman, Liz. "Dancing in Community: Its Roots in Art." Community Arts Network. Sep. 2002: http://www.communityarts.net/readingroom/archivefiles/2002/09/dancing_in_comm.php.

___. Interview with the author, Sept. 2008.

Putnam, Robert D., and Lewis M. Feldstein. "The Shipyard Project: Building Bridges with Dance." *Better Together: Restoring the American Community*. New York: Simon & Schuster, 2003.

Traiger, Lisa. "Making Dance That Matters: Dancer, Choreographer, Community Organizer, Public Intellectual Liz Lerman." Diss. (MA). University of Maryland, 2004.

Weeks, Janet. "When the Spirit Moves." *Dance Magazine* (Dec. 2006).

Liz Lerman Dance Exchange: http://www.danceexchange. org

JUDITH MARCUSE

Chodan, Lucinda. "Judith Marcuse's new dance company a family affair." *The Gazette* (Montréal), 10 Nov. 1984: C1.

Lazarus, John. "ICE: beyond belief." *Canadian Theatre Review* (Spring 2001).

Marcuse, Judith. Interview with the author, Oct. 2008.

Preston, Brian. "Dancing for Joy." *Imperial Oil Review* (Fall 1995).

Wachtel, Eleanor. "Moving Force." *Flare* (Sep. 1980).

Wyman, Max. *Revealing Dance: Selected Writings 1970's–2001*. Toronto: Dance Collection Press, 2001.

Dancing Full Out. Dir. Betsy Carson. Lodestar Productions, 2005. (Video)

Judith Marcuse, "Dancing Our Stories": http://people.uleth. ca/~scds.secd/dos/jmprinter.html.

International Centre of Art for Social Change (ICASC): http://www.icasc.ca/

ANNA PAVLOVA

Fonteyn, Margot. *The Magic of Dance*. New York: Alfred A. Knopf, 1979.

Fonteyn, Margot. *Pavlova: Impressions*. Eds. Roberta and John Lazzarini. London: Weidenfeld and Nicolson, 1984.

* Levine, Ellen. *Anna Pavlova: Genius of the Dance*. New York: Scholastic, 1995.

Oliphant, Betty. *Miss O: My Life in Dance*. Winnipeg: Turnstone, 1996.

* Pavlova, Anna. *I Dreamed I Was a Ballerina*. New York: Atheneum Books for Young Readers, 2001. (Text from Pavlova's 1922 autobiography, *Pages of My Life*, translated by Sebastien Voirol; illustrated with art by Edgar Degas.)

* Willson, Robina Beckles. *Anna Pavlova: A Legend Among Dancers*. London: Hodder and Stoughton, 1981.

PEARL PRIMUS

Foulkes, Julia L. *Modern Bodies: Dance and American Modernism from Martha Graham to Alvin Ailey*. Chapel Hill: University of North Carolina Press, 2002.

Kisselgoff, Anna. "Pearl Primus rejoices in the black tradition." *New York Times*, 19 June 1988.

Lloyd, Margaret. *The Borzoi Book of Modern Dance.* New York: Knopf, 1949.

Perpener III, John O. *African-American Concert Dance: The Harlem Renaissance and Beyond.* Urbana: University of Illinois Press, 2001.

Robertson, Michael. "Pearl Primus, PhD, returns." *New York Times,* 18 Mar. 1979: 34.

Public Broadcasting Service (PBS): http://www.pbs.org/wnet/freetodance/biographies/primus

Mamboso Nuyotopia: http://www.mamboso.net/primus/summary_2.html

ANNA SOKOLOW

Lloyd, Margaret. *The Borzoi Book of Modern Dance.* New York: Knopf, 1949.

Sokolow, Anna. "The Rebel and the Bourgeois." *The Modern Dance: Seven Statements of Belief.* Ed. Selma Jeanne Cohen. Middletown: Wesleyan University Press, 1966.

Sokolow, Anna. "The Dance." *Assignment in Israel.* Ed. Bernard Mandelbaum.

New York: Jewish Theological Seminary of America, 1960. 77–84.

Warren, Larry. *Anna Sokolow: The Rebellious Spirit.* Amsterdam: Harwood Academic Publishers, 1998 [1990].

Anna Sokolow: Choreographer. Dir. Lucille Rhodes and Margaret Murphy. First Dance Horizons, 1991 [1980]. (Video)

Jewish Women's Archive (JWA), "Anna Sokolow": http://www.jwa.org/exhibits.wov/sokolow

Sokolow Dance Foundation: http://www.annasokolow.org

JAWOLE WILLA JO ZOLLAR

Brennan, Lissa. "Urban Bush Women." *Essence* 33.5 (Sep. 2002): 112.

Kaufman, Sarah. "Urban Bush Women, celebrating Pearl Primus's 'Unquenched Fire.'" *Washington Post*, 27 Mar. 2006.

Shange, Ntozake. "Urban Bush Women: Dances for the Voiceless." *New York Times*. 8 Sep. 1991: 20.

Zollar, Jawole Willa Jo. Interview with the author, Aug. 2008.

Praise House. Dir. Julie Dash. KTCA-TV's Alive from Off-Center, 1991. (Video)

Public Broadcasting Service (PBS): http://www.pbs.org/wnet/freetodance/biographies/zollar.html

Urban Bush Women (UBW): http://www.urbanbushwomen.org.html

Photo Credits

cover:
Anna Pavlova: © New York Public Library
Geeta Chandran: courtesy Geeta Chandran
Carmen Amaya: © Hulton-Deutsch Collection/CORBIS
Karen Kain: Cylla von Tiedemann, courtesy The National Ballet of Canada

page 3: © New York Public Library
page 10: © New York Public Library
page 12: © New York Public Library

page 15: Martha Krueger, courtesy of the Sokolow Dance Foundation
page 16: courtesy of the Sokolow Dance Foundation
page 19: Alfredo Valente, courtesy of the Sokolow Dance Foundation
page 22: courtesy of the Sokolow Dance Foundation

page 27: © Hulton-Deutsch Collection/CORBIS
page 32: © Hulton-Deutsch Collection/CORBIS

Acknowledgments

Rona Arato, Sydell Waxman, Lynn Westerhout, and Frieda
Wishinsky
(My writing group)

Omayra Amaya
(Omayra Amaya Flamenco Dance Company)

Geeta and Rajiv Chandran
(Natya Vriksha Dance Company and School)

Carolyn Jackson, Melissa Kaita, Emma Rodgers, and Margie Wolfe
(Second Story Press)

Karen Kain, Adrienne Neville, and Pam Steele
(The National Ballet of Canada)

Liz Lerman, John Borstel, and Lee Woodman
(Liz Lerman Dance Exchange)

Judith and Richard Marcuse
(Judith Marcuse Projects)

Lorry May
(Sokolow Dance Foundation)

Peggy Schwartz
(Department of Music and Dance, University of Massachusetts,
Amherst, Massachusetts)

Jawole Willa Jo Zollar and Amy Cassello
(Urban Bush Women)